Outlaw Brand

DEKE FERGUSON

By

TRACY T. THURMAN

Copyright © 2018 Tracy T. Thurman

ISBN: 9781718077317

This is a work of fiction. Names, characters, businesses, places, events and incidents are either the products of the author's imagination or used in a fictitious manner. Any resemblance to actual persons, living or dead, or actual events is purely coincidental.

February 2018 First Edition

August 2018 Second Edition

This book is dedicated with respect, admiration, and gratitude to the many wonderful readers of American Western Fiction.

CHAPTER ONE

His mother named him Deacon. She thought a church name might ward off the demons. They called him Deke for short. She knew some men are branded at birth. She dreamed of a better life for him, something better than what he was born to. His mother's prayers must have been shot down like pie tins tossed in the air.

The Ferguson farm was situated on an unfortunate piece of ground. It was just far enough out of reach of good water and just close enough to nothing for it to bear anything but hardship and desperation. Even the rain showers that marched across the plains seemed to go out of their way to avoid the place.

Deke knelt in the hard scrabble dirt of his father's farm, clawing at the crusty soil to remove a large rock. His sixteen-year-old features were smudged with sweat and dust. He had the blonde hair and blue eyes of his mother's Scandinavian heritage. He wore an old tattered brown hat, threadbare overalls hung by one strap from a bony shoulder. His feet hadn't known shoes since the previous winter. He toiled endlessly in that unforgiving, often cruel patch of soil.

His task was to find and remove any obstruction that the plow share might encounter. A missed stone or large root would wreck the blade and bring down the old man's rage.

All too often Deke and his mother, Sarah, paid the price for David's temper. The farm drew the life out of those who worked it, giving scarce reward in return, what was left was made even harsher by David's heavy hand.

David struggled behind the mule, wrestling the plow into as straight a furrow as he could. His whiskered jaws clenched as the jostling contraption forced its way through the barren ground. Deke shuddered at the unmistakable screech of metal on stone. The sound caused an icy finger to run up his spine. He hung his head where he sat, knowing where the blame would fall.

David jerked the mule to a halt. Tossing the plow to its side he bent down to inspect the damage. A large gouge had been bent into the already worn out blade.

David's fists clenched the lines before he flung them to the ground. Fury swept over him.

"Dammit! Gawd awful Dammit!" He screamed.

Deke was already rising, resigned to his fate.

"C'mere, Deke!" the old man demanded.

The boy trudged over to his father, his eyes on the dirt at his feet knowing that by now the old man was already yanking a line off the damaged rig. When he got close enough David's hand shot out and clasped the boy's arm in a painful grip.

"You ain't worth half the price of this here blade! I'm gonna teach you once and for all if I have to beat you to death to do it!"

David jerked the boy around and raised the doubled over plow line. The lashes came sharp and cruel. Deke uttered not a sound as he fell under the whipping, doing his best to protect his face.

Sarah watched from the porch of the house, wringing her hands in her apron as her heart reached out to her son. She learned long ago that to interfere with David's anger would drive him into a blind rage, making matters much worse. Her pained gaze was drawn away suddenly by a horseman approaching at a gallop. His features could not be made out, but his form was familiar, and it terrified her.

David raised the line again as cruel welts raised on the boys back. Deke was doubled over on his knees, tensed for the next lash. The old man's arm froze in mid-swing when the gunshot cracked over his head.

The rider walked his horse to stand before the enraged man and the battered boy.

"I remember when Pa used to whip me like that. I always wished someone would come along and shoot the son-of-a-bitch for me!"

David scowled at the man who sat aboard the broad chested black. The sun was at the man's back and he had to squint to see his face, but David knew who the intruder was.

"Maybe if Pa had a whipped you a little harder and a little longer you wouldn't be the theivin', murder'n trash you are, Carl!"

The man sneered in contempt at the remark as he replaced the spent shell, spinning the cylinder back in place and holstered the gun, he answered with a bellowing laugh.

"Now, Davy boy, that ain't no way to greet your long lost big brother is it? Besides, I was just wonderin' if beatin' up on scrawny boys was how you honest folks make your livin' or is it just somethin' ya do for fun?"

David threw the plow line to the ground. "What do you want Carl?"

Carl eyed the boy as he staggered to his feet and then shifted a severe glare back toward David. The two men exchanged an uneasy silent moment. Hatred lived between them. Though they shared the same blood, Carl and David Ferguson were contemptuous of each other. Both men had grown under the stern and often brutal hand of their father and wore their bitterness outwardly. Carl was the bigger of the two.

Both men had dark complexions and were broad shouldered. David appeared older and always considered himself the better of the two, yet neither man had ever escaped the harsh lessons of their youth. They simply employed them in different ways.

"I'm just passin through here, thought I'd drop by and visit and maybe get a drink of water, that is, if you got any water around this place." Carl replied with disdain as he looked about the area.

"We got water. Deke, go and fetch him up a drink, but don't bother visitin' 'cause your uncle Carl here ain't staying long, not even long enough to get out of that fancy saddle he probably stole." David's eyes were hard and filled with scorn, his voice carrying an edge of venom. Carl smiled sideways and reined his horse around toward the well.

Sarah stood halfway behind the door eyeing the big man with the horror of a terrible secret screaming within her.

Deke pulled a bucket from the well and grabbed a tin cup to hand up to the man on the horse. Carl nodded and said thanks, looking in to the pain-filled face of the boy as he drank. Handing the cup back he reached down and ruffled the boy's hair, offering him a genuine smile in return. Deke brightened up and held the bucket to the big black's nose.

"Deacon is it?"

"Yes, sir. They call me Deke." He replied, glancing cautiously at the old man standing hands on hips in the field.

"Your pa whip you a lot like that?"

"Just when he gets real mad."

"Bet he gets mad quite often, don't he?"

Deke's eyes went to the ground. "Yes, sir."

"You want me to shoot him for you?"

Deke looked back up suddenly, Carl was grinning at the question. The boy didn't answer.

"Deke!" David's yell came from across the field.

"I'd better git."

Carl looked out and glared again at his brother. "Alright, good talkin' to ya, Deke. I'll see ya 'round."

The big man smiled again at the boy and pulled the black back toward the distance. He paused for a moment at the front of the house, somber faced, he looked at Sarah as she peered out from behind the door. He tipped his hat and trotted away. She slammed the door.

Sarah moved back into the house. Falling into a chair she buried her face in her hands. The horrid memories came back to her. She trembled, feeling sick to her stomach, as they unfolded in her mind.

It was that night, that terrible night more than sixteen years before when David left her alone to go to Silver Springs. He had to go for the title of the farm and to buy things they would need as they started their lives together. The darkness, the wind and the driving rain, the thunder and lightning of that night made her so afraid. It was an evil storm.

The storm delivered a drunken Carl Ferguson to her doorstep. He forced himself in, bleary-eyed and salivating. The stench of his whiskey soaked breath was still clear in her mind.

She tried to fight, oh how she tried. Carl was relentless in his lust and complete in his use of her. He stayed until the next day, taking her at his will, heavy handed and malicious he forced her to endure unspeakable things.

She recalled how she raised her battered face from the floor, bruised and hurt, her dress torn to shreds around her. She begged him to kill her. She pleaded with him through her sobs not to force her to live with the shame and the terror.

He pushed her away with the toe of his boot. Telling her she chose the wrong brother and laughed at her agony.

She had no recollection of his leaving. She passed out there after and awoke in the darkness, lying in a heap on the floor, a cold draft and ray of moonlight entering through the open door.

She put herself back together as best she could. There was no way she could have told David. She fabricated a story of being thrown from the mare. It had cost the old horse her life, but it was a sacrifice that Sarah had to make. "Why was he back? Oh, Lord, why!?"

She began to swell with motherhood soon thereafter. Whether the new life growing within her was born of the seed of her husband or her violent brother-in-law, she would not ever know for certain, and she would not admit her suspicions even to herself.

******

The stillness in the Ferguson house was like death that night. Deke sat backwards in a chair resting his chin on his folded arms while his mother smeared salve on the welts that crossed his back. He winced now and then but showed no other sign. He stood tall to David's abuse. Even if not in a physical way, he did so mentally out of sheer determination. Courage fueled by hatred is a formidable defense.

David tossed his dinner plate into the wash basin and stomped across the room sucking his teeth as he went. Picking up his smoking material and a bottle from the cabinet he paused only long enough to glare at the woman and the boy before stepping outside.

"Someday I'm gonna kill that man." Deke said while glaring at the door. Sarah gasped and spun him around to face her. Hatred had brought alive the meanness that was born within him. She recoiled at the flame that now danced wickedly in her son's eyes. Her lips trembled, and she struggled to speak but no words came to her. She clasped the boy in her arms and tried her best to choke back the tears from the breaking of her heart.

She hoped that Deke would be spared the malice that seemed to be the trait of the Ferguson men. She blamed herself for allowing it to happen and for bringing this boy into a world that knew little else than cruelty.

"Please don't think like that, or ever say things like that." She implored.

Deke pushed away and looked into her eyes, "Why do you care? The way he treats us...? I'd be doing you a favor."

She studied the question in his eyes for a moment. "It is not him I am concerned with. It is you and where those kinds of thoughts and actions will take you."

Deke shrugged, "I guess it would take us both away from here." He responded.

She pressed her hands firmly against his shoulders emphasizing her emotion as she spoke sternly but quietly. "Son, you have never known kindness the way I wish you had, but hatred and brutality will only lead you down the road to becoming the very thing you hate."

Deke shrugged again, a loathing sneer curling his lip. "I'll never be like that man there." He said.

The sun was halfway up when David loaded the wounded plow into the buck board. "I'm headed to Silver Springs to try to make a deal on a new one or at least get this one fixed." He climbed into the seat and gathered up the reins. "Try and get some work done while I'm gone."

Deke nodded but didn't say a word. He was just glad to see the old man gone for a couple of days. He walked into the house and closed the door behind him. Sarah was busy at the kitchen counter cleaning up the breakfast dishes. "I'm gonna go down to the creek and do some fishing." He said.

"You need to clean the barn out first. You know what your father said." She warned.

Deke shook his shoulders in defiance. "Hell with him." He spat.

Sarah turned from her work and eyed him with disapproval. "I'll not have you talking like that in this house!" she scolded. "Now get out there and clean that barn!"

He nodded and strode toward the barn. She watched him through the window as he went. Her hands twisting the dish towel fretfully. It was too late to avoid his fate. She knew it now.

Deke raked and forked the stalls and straightened the gear that hung about the place. He was coiling a rope when a movement caught the corner of his eye.

Moving to investigate he caught sight of a rat scurrying behind a grain box. He reached for a spade that stood nearby and stalked the rodent into a corner. The rat made a move to the side and Deke brought the spade down hard upon it. The creature flailed and squealed from the blow. He brought the point of the spade down to rest against its neck. He pressed slowly. Something dark swelled up inside the boy as he watched the rodent writhe and struggle in vain. Finally, the rat's instinct to survive was spent; the pathetic creature looked up at its assailant as its life slipped away, it convulsed and lay dead.

He stood and looked at the rat. Only moments before it had been a living thing and now by a simple turn of his hand he had taken its life away.

He left the rat lying in place and gathered his fishing gear, but before he left, he went over to it again and nudged the lifeless thing with his toe. He turned away with a feeling of dark satisfaction.

The creek was a thin tributary that ran cool and clear most of the time. The banks were steep and wooded. Deke stretched out and watched his line hang limp in the water. He heard a movement behind him and stood up quickly.

"Howdy, Deke." The big man leaned against a tree twirling a twig in his teeth.

Deke was surprised by the sudden appearance of his uncle Carl. He looked around not knowing whether to run or stay.

Carl tossed the twig away and smiled. "Don't worry, boy, I'm not gonna hurt ya. I'm just here to visit and maybe get to know ya a little better."

Deke relaxed a bit. He liked this man that his father hated. "I was just doin' a little fishin'." was all he could say in reply.

Carl laughed and strode over to where Deke was and sat on the bank of the creek. He paused for a moment and began tossing pebbles into the water.

"Nothing wrong with a little fishin'." Carl replied smiling, then looked over at the youngster.

"Ya'know, we're family, me and you and I sure hate to see ya get used up on that old farm. If ya wanna call it that..."

Deke sat down and listened.

"Me and your pa, well, we never did see things quite the same. I'm a thinkin' you're a pretty smart boy, too smart to spend your days scratchin' in the dirt and getting whipped like a dog."

Deke looked down and nodded. "The old man gets mad a lot." He said, thinking of the painful welts across his back.

Carl looked over and smiled. "How'd you like to work for me and earn a few dollars?"

Deke never had any money of his own and the prospect of it sounded good. "What do I have to do?"

Carl laughed again. "That a boy, straight to the point. I need a couple, three head of cows and a good rider with a keen eye to find some and drive 'em out to me over by the buttes. You think you could do that?"

"I don't have a horse or nothin' and I ain't never…"

Carl held his hand up. "I'll leave ya a horse right over there tonight if you think you can sneak away and get the job done."

Deke looked over to where Carl pointed. "Yes, sir, I think I can."

"All right then. But ya can't tell your folks or anybody else. This is strictly business between you and me."

Carl stood, prompting Deke to do the same. The big man offered his hand. "Do we got a deal?"

Deke shook his hand "Yes, sir!"

That night, he lay awake until the moon was high. He crept out and ran to the place where the horse would be tied. It was a strong, well conformed animal, much different than the scrawny old sorrel mare they used on the farm.

The bay gelding lifted his head in alarm as Deke approached but quickly settled down as it sniffed his out-stretched hand. It pawed the ground and bobbed its head tired of being tied and eager to get on the trail. Deke swung up in the saddle and reined the animal around. Trotting off into the night, he didn't realize then that the trail he picked that night would lead him in a much different direction than just after a few stray cows.

The ranch down the road had hundreds of cattle and Deke was sure he could round up a few and trail them off to where Carl said.

He rode off the trail and within a couple hours he managed to find four good yearlings that were laying low in the brush for the night. He gathered them up walking the horse in a circle around them, then holding behind them, pushed them along.

The buttes weren't much more than a cluster of hills that rose up out of the prairie. Heavily wooded and irregular, they were a natural maze of small valleys and hiding places. Deke pushed his catch toward them.

While Deke was engaged in his new enterprise Carl had an errand of his own.

*****

Carl ambled the big black up to the house and sat there in front of the door. He thought of stepping up on the porch and knocking, but then thought better of it. He cleared his throat loudly.

The door opened, and the barrel of a gun protruded from it. Sarah's voice was shaking but stern. "Come any closer and I'll kill you!"

Carl sat still but raised his hands, palms out. "Now, Sarah, I just want to talk to ya a minute." He said calmly.

"You've got some nerve!" She hissed. "You better hope David doesn't wake up and come out here and shoot you himself!"

Carl paused, then replied, "I know that David ain't here, Sarah." He looked away then back to her again his head hanging low as he spoke.

"Sarah, I'm sorry for what I done to you. I was crazy and drunk. When you married David, I lost my mind."

Sarah drew back as though his words were the gravest of insults.

"You son-of- a- bitch! I hate you and I will kill you if you don't leave here right now!"

Carl stared directly at her.

"I gotta know, Sarah...?"

"You gotta know what?! Whose son he is?! He is MY son! Mine! And between the Ferguson brothers he's all but out of chances to have a decent life!"

Sarah swung the door wide then and stepped out in full view, her fear had turned to anger, and now at the mention of her son it had turned to rage. She held the pistol steady, aimed at the middle of Carl's chest.

Carl looked away then back again. "Why don't you come away with me?" He asked. "Let me put you up in a real house and get that boy some real schoolin'."

"HA!" Sarah laughed. "You are trash, Carl Ferguson, you will burn in hell for what you've done to me and God knows who else! I only wish I could be there to see it! Now get out of here and don't you ever come back! You stay away from my son!"

Carl nodded and took up the reins, "All right, but I ain't gonna let that husband of yours treat that boy like that. I aim to give him a chance."

Sarah cocked the hammer back, "Leave!" she demanded.

*****

"Hold up there!" The gruff voice came from out of the darkness. Deke pulled up and strained his eyes to see the man who had spoken. "You Carl's nephew?"

"Yes, sir, I'm Deke Ferguson and I'm bringin' in a few head of cattle for him."

He sat up straight in the saddle intentionally deepening his voice as he spoke.

A man suddenly appeared out of the shadows. He carried a rifle across his chest and walked toward the boy and the milling steers.

"Well! Looks like ya done a fair job, young man." The man said then offered up his hand. "I'm Slate. That's what folks call me."

Deke shook Slate's hand and introduced himself again. "I'm Deke, good to meet you, Mister Slate."

"Nah, no mister, just Slate." the man grinned, then motioned ahead toward a turn in the trail. "Let's git em up there and settle up. Carl oughta be back soon, but either way you'll need to get goin'."

The two pushed the cattle into a small canyon that curved out and back again from the trail. There were about thirty or forty more head and they turned the new arrivals in with them.

Slate reached in his pocket and pulled out a folded pack of bills. "Let's see here…"

The man eyed the bills and looked over at Deke. "You brought in three steers…"

"No, Sir. I brought in four." Deke corrected him holding up four fingers.

"Ha ha! You're right, yep, sure enough, four it was. I just wanted to see if you were easy to fool." the man chuckled. "So, that's four good steers, at a dollar apiece, that makes four dollars." He counted out the money and handed it to Deke.

The boy's eyes were wide. Four dollars to him might as well been all the money in the world. For a few hours work he got paid more than he had ever seen in a lifetime.

He tried not to act excited and held himself in check. "Thank you." He said.

"Sure enough. Well, Deke, you'd better git back. Take the horse and leave it where ya found it. We'll take care of it. I'll make sure and tell Carl what a top hand and smart businessman you are."

Deke swung in to the saddle and grinned as he rode away. Four dollars!

When he got home the eastern sky was growing light. He tiptoed across the porch and eased the door open. He was startled to find Sarah sleeping in a chair with a large pistol held in her lap. She jerked awake when his foot landed on a squeaking board. Her eyes narrowed as she looked at him. "Where have you been?" she demanded.

Deke told her that he had stayed at the creek, that he had fallen asleep there. She didn't believe him. Deke eyed the gun in Sarah's hand.

"What's that for?"

"It's for varmints and rabid dogs and other critters that sneak around in the middle of the night." She said scornfully.

She walked across the room and placed the gun in a drawer in the kitchen counter.

Deke pulled it back out and studied it.

"It was my father's." She said. "It's a Colt Navy .44. I don't know where he got it, but he gave it to me just after me and your father were married."

Deke looked at the big pistol and back to her again. "Why?"

Sarah shrugged. "Guess he thought I oughta have it." She answered then took the gun from Deke's hands and placed it again in the drawer. As she laid it down she quietly thought of all the times she could have used it.

David would return that evening, so Deke hustled to get done the things that might show the old man he had been busy. He might come back with a new plow, but he would certainly come back with a new bottle. If he started on that when he was already mad, there would be hell to pay and Deke and Sarah would foot the bill.

He was spading weeds when he caught the glimpse of something shining from the creek. He dropped the shovel and went to investigate.

Carl was there shining a small mirror to get his attention. Deke walked up the man. "I see you make a pretty fair cattleman." Carl said as the boy approached.

"I just found some cows and drove 'em out to you like you said."

Carl smiled and nodded. "Well, that's about all there is to it." He said then continued. "Say, me and a few of my associates have a little work to do tonight. I wonder if you might want to come along and help out?"

Deke thought of David's return, but thought again of the easy money that a few head of stray cows had brought. "Alright." He replied plainly.

"I'll leave your horse right where he was last night. I'll see ya then." Carl swung into the saddle and rode off. Deke returned to his spade and thought of making money enough to gather himself and his mother and leave this place and the old man for good.

David arrived just before sundown. The old plow share had been repaired but was still the same old worn out contraption. Sarah met David in front of the house eyeing the contents of the wagon. "I thought you were going to try to get a new one."

David's expression was angry. "Oh, that man at the store said that my credit wasn't good, and I didn't have enough to outright buy one." David flung the ropes away from the wagon and lifted out a box of goods that Sarah had asked for. "Imagine that fat sumbitch tellin' me my credit ain't good!" The more he thought about it the madder he got. In the box was a new bottle of cheap whiskey. It was going to be a long night.

When the ruckus from his parent's bedroom stopped and he finally heard David's guttural snores, Deke slipped out and ran to where the horse would be tied. He wasted no time, leaped into the saddle, and headed for the buttes. Slate met him on the road and guided him to the other men. There were three others besides Carl.

All sat horses that were tall and strong, animals that would be the envy of any horseman, unless of course he was standing in the presence of Carl's big black.

"Howdy Deke!" Carl greeted then made a motion to the others. "Boys, this here is my, uh… nephew, Deke Ferguson. Deke this here is Bill Sinclair" He said pointing to a sour faced, pot-bellied man with a beard. "This here is Bobby Smith." He said indicating a younger man, not much older than Deke was himself. Bobby lifted a hand and grinned with crooked teeth. "And this homely hombre is Cotton Joe." He indicated a lean tough looking man with dark eyes who slowly nodded making no other expression. "And I guess you already know Slate."

Deke nodded at the group and took note of Bill Sinclair's obvious disdain. The older man nodded curtly in Deke's direction and spat a stream of tobacco juice.

They rode quietly until they came to a line of trees that overlooked the stage depot. "Ya see them horses down there?" Carl whispered pointing at the corral.

"The stage line dropped them off yesterday and I figure we need them worse than they do." The others chuckled lowly at the statement. "Now we're gonna ride down there and bring them horses up. All you gotta do is stand watch and hold Bobby's horse."

Bill spoke up. "What about the station agent?" He asked.

Carl looked over at him with a wry smile. "Oh, him? Well ya see, that fellar is a family man, and, well, he and I have what ya might call an agreement. I think he had to take his misses over to the next county for a few days to visit an ailing sister or somethin'." Carl winked as he finished his story. The others chuckled.

Bobby stepped down from the saddle and handed the reins to Deke and taking a hackamore in hand swung up on the back of Slate's horse. Deke nodded and watched as the men spurred their mounts toward the corral.

When they reached the place, Bobby jumped from Slate's horse and leaped over the rail. He quickly secured the hackamore around the head of one of the horses, swung the gate open, jumped astride and circled the corral pushing the others out.

The other horses followed and soon the bunch were high-tailing it out and up to where Deke sat.

Bobby hopped off the stolen animal and back into his own saddle as Deke handed him back his reins. They kicked the animals into a run and headed back to where they came from.

Excitement rose in Deke's heart as they went thundering through the moonlit night.

He rode alongside the pack just to Carl's right. Carl glanced over at him and grinned proudly. They bunched the horses up in a different canyon from where the cattle were and walked their horses to cool them down.

Carl sat and counted. "That's twenty-six good mounts boys!" He said cheerfully. "Not a bad night's work."

Bill Sinclair pulled up alongside. "You're plumb loco Carl, bringin' that kid along."

Carl smirked back at him, "You let me worry about who I bring along and who I don't, Bill." He replied flatly. He was not in the habit of explaining his actions and saw no reason to do so now.

Deke felt good in the presence of these men. Like he belonged with them, "How much you think they're worth?" He asked. Bill Sinclair scoffed at the boy's question.

Carl shot a mean glance his way then looked back at Deke. "Oh, I don't know for sure, horses like these don't draw top dollar ya' know. But they'll pay."

Carl pointed to Slate. "Hey, Slate, pay this man for his work so's he can get back before there's trouble for him."

Slate reached in his pocket and counted out five dollars. "Here ya go, Deke. 'Preciate your help." Deke took the money, wide-eyed, folded it up and placed it in his pocket.

Carl winked at him and said. "Good work, Deke, you're gonna shape into a good hand." Bill Sinclair scoffed again and spat a stream of tobacco juice. Deke glared back at him this time. Bill's contempt was obvious, and Deke was not afraid to return it.

Deke tied the horse to a branch and hurried back to the house. He slipped in the door taking care to avoid the creaky board from the night before. A match flared suddenly, and the room grew bright. David sat shirtless in a chair at the kitchen table, a half empty bottle in his hand. He turned up the wick in the lantern and glared at him. "Where you been, boy?" He asked. His voice was thick with whisky.

Deke trembled as he faced the old man. "I was out at the barn." He said, trying to think fast.

The old man slammed the bottle on the table. "You're a liar!" He shouted. "I been out at the barn and I didn't see you anywhere!" The old man scowled rising from his chair. "Now I'm gonna ask you again, boy. Where you been?!"

Deke's face flushed red hot. He was caught and there was no escape. "I been out chasin' horses and got paid better money than you'll ever see to do it!" He spat.

David yanked the belt from around his waist, whipping it through his belt loops, anger swelled up into rage. "You been gettin' mighty big for your britches, boy. I'm gonna teach you the way of things if I have to beat you into the ground!" He raised his arm with the doubled-over belt hanging from his hand. Deke tensed, but stood firm.

"No, you are not!" Sarah's voice came from behind as she entered the room. "No. you are not!" she repeated. "You'll not beat that boy anymore!"

Her hand caught David's arm. He cursed her and swung his hand in a vicious blow that sent her reeling. She caught herself and lunged back, teeth gritted, grasping for the belt!

David roared and cursed her again. His big hand grabbed her under the chin, then he flung her across the room as though she were a rag doll. Sarah flailed trying to catch herself, she stumbled over a chair. Her head struck the corner of the kitchen counter with a sickening crack. Sarah screamed, a short, cut-off kind of scream of pain and fear as she fell to the floor.

Deke's eyes were wide, and his heart seemed to stop in his chest. He rushed over and knelt beside his mother. Blood flowed freely from her scalp and pooled beneath her head. She gazed up at him briefly, her lips moved in an odd way, but no sound came forth. Sarah twitched for a moment, gasped and lay still. Deke looked into his mother's eyes and saw the light and the life fade away from them.

David looked down her. "Sarah?" He said. "Sarah!" He knelt beside her shaking her, but her body was limp and lifeless. He glared at Deke, grabbing him by the nape of the neck he shoved the boy across the room. "This never would have happened had you been where you were supposed to be!" He yelled.

Deke stumbled and glared back at him. David stood over Sarah's body shaking his head and cursing. He turned only when he heard Deke's voice.

There was something low and cold that David had not heard before. He looked and saw Deke standing with the Colt his mother had placed in the drawer. His face was red, his eyes tear-filled and narrowed in hatred, "I always wished someone would come along and shoot the son-of- a-bitch for me." He repeated Carl's words as he brought the weapon to bear.

"Now see here, boy!" David pointed a shaky finger. Deke pulled the trigger. The gun boomed in the confines of the house. The bullet struck David high in the chest sending him toppling over the table, knocking the lamp to the floor where it crashed into pieces.

Flaming oil spread quickly in the room. David gasped and grunted trying to crawl away.

Deke stepped over to where David lay, shoving the upturned table aside as he did so. He aimed the gun at David's forehead. David glared up at him. "I should of whipped you longer and harder." The big gun boomed again, and David sprawled dead in the burning wreckage of the house.

Deke stared at the lifeless forms of his parents, standing amid the flames as the fire grew and enveloped their bodies. Finally, the heat and the smoke drove him out. He staggered as if in a trance stepping over the squeaky board as he made his way through the wreckage and closed the door behind him.

He turned in a daze to face the house, watching the building and all he knew become consumed. The flames grew large, roaring and twisting violently as though the fire had a life and will of its own.

The sound of running hooves came from behind him, but he did not turn. He stood mesmerized by the flames. The gun hung in his hand at his side. Tears fell but dried; a chill swept through him.

Carl leapt down from the saddle and took Deke by the shoulders. "What happened here?" He asked.

Deke relayed the story and pointed to the burning house as it collapsed in upon itself. "They're inside."

Carl looked at the boy and back at the house. He shook his head. "I guess David had it comin', I sure feel bad about your ma though." Deke looked up at him. "Don't." He said.

They stood and watched for a moment. When the porch roof fell in, Carl laid a hand on Deke's shoulder. "You got a horse in that barn?"

"Just that old sorrel." He replied.

"Well, you'd better get it and whatever else you can find to take. I figure you just as well come with me."

Deke lifted his hand that held the pistol and then looked up at Carl. "I think this is all." He said.

The two rode out together, the roar of the fire jeered at them as they left, the flames danced tauntingly behind their backs.

Tracy T. Thurman

CHAPTER TWO

It wasn't a long ride, but one that put enough distance behind them for the great tension in Deke's body to subside. His shoulders slumped, and he suddenly felt very tired.

When they rode into the outlaw camp a man standing watch hollered out. The gang met them as they reined in. Deke sat still, smoke smudged and dirty. His eyes were red rimmed as he glanced about.

Carl sat aboard his horse as the men gathered around and motioned to the boy.

"Boys, this here is Deacon Ferguson. We call him Deke. He'll be ridin' with us from here on out. I want ya'll to show him the ropes and how we do things in this operation. He is my blood, but he gets no special favors and don't ride him because of it either."

The men in the gang all mumbled a welcome and took turns introducing themselves. All except for Bill Sinclair. "I ain't here to nurse maid no kid!" He spat.

Carl eyed him angrily. "Nobody asked ya to, Bill!" He spat in return. Carl looked at the men before him and dismounted. Deke did the same. "It's about time we wrap this up and head out. We got stock to sell and goods to swap. Now ya'll get to work. Bobby, take Deke over to Flap Jacks and get him fed. Rustle around and see if we can't find some decent duds for him until he can get some of his own."

Bobby cocked his head over toward the chuck wagon. "C'mon, Deke, I'll get ya set up and get ya some grub."

Carl motioned to Slate and pulled him off to the side. He spoke deliberately but quietly, explaining the recent events. "I want you to take one other man and go out there to that house and give them folks a decent burial." Slate nodded solemnly and turned to go when Carl caught him, "Separate graves." He added, then softly spoke another few words before sending him on his way.

The chuck wagon was a stripped down version of a standard cattleman's conveyance. It was relieved of extra weight and non-essential equipment. The wheels were reinforced as were the springs, axles, and tongue.

Carl had it built for fast travel in rough country. It was sturdy, and rugged as any old chuck wagon would be as they were meant to be home and hearth for cowboys on the range. The needs of an outfit that ran on the outside of the law however called for a slightly different design and utility. Carl wanted to be sure that his outfit could pack up and move as swiftly as possible.

Leaving a bogged down or broken wagon behind would mean losing a lot of their gains and gear. Carl designed the wagon well.

Flap Jacks Johnson was tall and thin, formerly a buffalo soldier with a childhood as a house servant on a southern plantation. He had found life among the law abiding folks was difficult and lacking in promise.

Most people had not yet become accustomed to having his kind among them and the struggle to fit in or at least get an even break was finally more than he was willing to endure.

He was a vicious fighter who was known as much for his skill with a knife as for his quick sense of humor and easy laugh. An Apache lance had ruined his right knee during his Army days. They gave him a medal and a steel leg brace for his service.

His disability precluded him from being an effective horseman, his skill as a cook, however, fitted him perfectly for tending the chuck wagon. He considered it a fine job, in that he got an even share in the gang's profits and didn't have to get shot at in the process.

Flap Jacks was rolling a tarp and packing his gear when Bobby and Deke strode up to the wagon. He stood up and eyed the two youngsters as they approached. "What you got there, Bobby?"

Bobby motioned at his companion, "This here is Deke. He's gonna be ridin' with us."

Flap Jacks looked at the frail boy before him and placed his hands on his hips.

"Boy, you look like you ain't ate in a week! You ain't sickly is ya?"

Deke shook his head staring wide-eyed at the man before him. He had never encountered such a man before. Flap Jacks pulled his head back and returned his stare. "Wha's a matter boy? Ain't you never seen a man handsome as me befo'?"

He glared back at the boy for a moment, then laughed loudly, his big grin disarming the youngster, causing him and Bobby to laugh in return. Laughter was an odd experience for Deke.

Bobby placed a hand on his shoulder. "Deke, this here is Flap Jacks Johnson." He told him. "He's the cook, barber, and doctor of the outfit. He'll even sew on a button for ya if ya need it, just be careful of his biscuits. ya might chip a tooth. You'll be helping him out for a while at least until ya get settled in or we find somethin' better for ya to do."

Flap Jacks scoffed at the comment. "It'll be 'bout time I had some help around here!" He looked at Deke. "These lazy no-accounts can't even wipe they own chins!" He glared back at Bobby, amused at the exchange.

There was a large pot of beef and beans simmering next the fire. The aroma attracted Deke's senses, he suddenly realized the ravenous hunger that gnawed at his stomach. He felt weak and trembled as if cold.

"Grab yo-sef a plate from over there and spoon ya up some of that grub. It's jus' gonna get throwed out anyhow."

Deke took a large metal plate from the shelf in the wagon and scooped it full from the pot. He sat in the shade of the wagon and began shoveling large spoonful's of the food into his mouth. He barely got a mouth full chewed before shoving in the next bite. Bobby and Flap Jacks watched him in awe for a moment, exchanging glances.

Deke felt a bump on his shoulder. He looked up and saw Flap Jack's long, thin arm handing a cup of water to him. "Betta wash some of it down. You're liable to choke."

Deke took the cup and gulped the water down. Flap Jacks refilled it and handed it back, shaking his head.

A bundle fell at his feet as he was sopping up the last of the meal with a biscuit.

Bobby squatted down before him. "Here's some old clothes I kept from last year. They got to snug for me. They might fit ya. Don't worry, they're clean." He said.

Deke looked up from his empty plate, "Thank you." He said to both men. He stood as Flap Jacks took his plate. "I'll clean these for ya this time, but from here on out your gonna be doing the washin'." He said with a big grin.

Deke shook out the clothes that Bobby had given him. A pair of old Levis. a blue button down shirt, a pair of boots that, though worn, were a sight better than any he'd ever had.

He began to pull off his old clothes when he heard Flap Jacks loudly clear his throat. Deke looked over and saw the man's scowling expression as he held out a bar of soap and a towel. Flap Jacks said not a word but motioned the creek with a nod of his head. Deke took the hint and the soap and headed to the water.

After bathing he changed into the new clothes. He turned away as he went to put on the shirt. Flap Jacks noticed the scars across the boys back. He knew right away what caused scars like that. He shook his head.

Deke felt a foot taller in the boots and the clothes fit him well. A bit loose but not so much as to hang off. He felt as though he'd come into a life where living was much more than simply toiling in the dirt. A new excitement welled up in him. It was something he had never felt before.

"Now you might be fit to be around decent folks!" Flap Jacks laughed when he rounded the wagon and tossed Deke's old clothes on the fire. The cook was holding the old pistol Deke had brought with him, examining it interestedly. "Now why you totin' a hog laig like dis here?" He asked.

Deke stepped up to him and withdrew the gun from the man's hands. "It was my ma's. She kept it for varmints and rabid dogs and other critters that sneak around in the night." He repeated her words like lines from a play.

Flap Jacks stuck his lip out in consideration of the statement. "You got two fired charges there. You gonna reload it?"

Deke had very little idea of firearms. He shrugged his shoulders. "I reckon."

The cook eyed him suspiciously. "You know how to load that thang?"

Deke paused, embarrassed by his lack of knowledge. The cook dug into a small trunk in the back of the wagon. "I got me some powder and ball in here that I keep for my own. Brang that iron over and we'll load it."

He handed the pistol to the man and watched as he deftly charged the two empty chambers. Taking an oil cloth from the wagon he handed it over to Deke. "Now wrap that up in here and put it with your other gear. She'll be ready for ya if ya need her again."

Deke did as he was instructed and placed the bundle in the wagon next to the blankets he was given. Flap Jacks nodded at him. "Ya oughta git yosef' a better gun, one that pulls a little quicker and loads a might easier."

"I will"

"Now... gimme a hand and les' git dis here rig packed up." Flap Jacks said.

As the two worked Deke watched with interest as the lithe man completed his chores. He was tall and broad chested, amiable with a strength in his arms that could easily be twice that of others. He was the cook, but he did not look the part.

"Why do they call you Flap Jacks?"

The man paused and looked quizzically at the boy. "Why not?" He answered.

"Lot's a folks go by different han'les in these parts." Deke tossed off the comment, but his question still hung in the air.

Flap Jacks sat back on the ground where he was packing supplies in a large bundle.

"Wa'll ya see when I was a youngster I worked in a big plantation. I worked in the house and helped with the cookin' and such. The man who ran the house was a mean old cuss and treated folks real bad. They was a woman and a boy there. He liked to smack that woman around and he was downright cruel to dat boy. They was friends of mine, as much as the white folk could have been in that place an' time. Wa'll the old man was partial to Flap Jacks and one day he got real sick and died. Folks say he must a got poisoned or somethin'. They say I did it and was gonna hang me. Wa'll that boy come out to where they had me all shackled up and turned me loose. His ma give me a hoss and some food and a letter and told me to light out west and find a Captain that had their same last name. So, I did. They was nice folks."

Deke looked interested at hearing the story. "Did ya?" He asked.

"Did I what?"

"Did ya poison the old man?"

A crooked smile turned up the corner of Flap Jacks' lip.

"Now I ain't gonna say I did or I didn't, but dat mean old sumbitch shore didn't bother dat woman or dat boy no mo'!"

Later that day Slate, soot covered and dirty, tied his horse and walked up to Carl.

He dug in his pocket and dropped a small, but tarnished ring into Carl's hand. "Just as you said, separate graves. There weren't much left, them oak floors burn mighty hot. He sure did it for his old man though. Blew the top of his head clean off."

Carl's face grew dark at the explanation and Slate immediately wished he hadn't spoken so freely.

Carl nodded. "Thanks." He said and slapped Slate on the shoulder. Slate nodded in reply and taking his horse walked down to the stream to clean up. The odor of death was still on him and right then he wanted nothing more in the world than to be shed of it.

The drive away from the buttes took the outfit North and East. They camped along the way. Deke gathered firewood and fetched water for the chuck wagon. He scrubbed pots and pans. Flap Jacks kept him busy. He slept under the wagon, rolled tight in his blankets sweating profusely regardless of the chill in the air.

His mind replayed the recent events. Fire raged in his dreams, his mother's cries and his father's curses emanated from within the flames. He felt again, and again the recoil of the pistol in his hand. Deke's first few nights of his new life were fitful. Flap Jacks lifted himself from his bedroll and leaned on an elbow. He watched the boy thrash about, heard his mumbling, and shook his head. "Dat boy gonna have a hard life." He said to himself and laid his head back down staring up the stars.

He had his own nightmares, though they had mercifully faded over the years, and he'd heard those of others; fighting and struggling in their sleep from far away battles that scarred a man's soul as much as his flesh. They were the dreams of grown men, who had seen and done the worst of things. They should not be the dreams of the young.

They were up and moving at first light. Tall stands of timber grew larger as they went. They avoided roads and common trails. They finally ended up at what they called the "Home Place". It was a large canyon with trees and grass, and plenty of water supplied by the wide stream that flowed through the center of it. The entrance was a gap, formed by two ridges coming together. A long road lead to it. Inside, the ground sloped down into a bowl of sorts. It flowed inward, leveled off and spilled out between another, wider, gap on the opposite corner.

High up against the canyon wall, where the ground rose again, a cabin stood. Flanked by trees and rock, it was built solid with large pine logs. It had a wide porch, the posts of which still had some of the bark on them. You had to be careful leaning against them because of the sap that oozed out on warm days.

Other cabins lay here and there, a long bunk house to one side housed most of the hands while the other smaller ones held supplies and equipment.

Flap Jacks had his own cabin that had a place for a kitchen garden and where the chuck wagon was kept when not out on the trail. It was not a residence that reflected any prejudice one way or the other, just an arrangement of convenience so that the hours and duties the cook kept didn't interfere with those of the rest of the outfit.

Bill Sinclair had his own cabin as did Slate. Such were the benefits of their rank within the operation. Bobby stayed in the bunkhouse with the others. Deke was told to put up in a back room of Flap Jacks' cabin as he would mostly be working the kitchen chores when not working as an extra hand in other endeavors.

One night, when Flap Jacks had wrestled the big leather straps away from his leg and pulled the steel brace painfully away. Deke asked him about his injury. The brace fell with a thud to the floor next to Flap Jacks' bunk.

The man looked away, staring into his memories. "We was in Arizona territory, the 'Paches was off the rez and actin up. Raidin' folks and causin' all kinds of trouble.

The Cap'n said we was to round 'em up or kill 'em, didn't matter which to him, so longs we got 'em settled down." He reached under his bunk and drew out a bottle, uncorked it and took a long drink, his adam's apple bobbed as he swallowed. "I was a sergeant and was leading a patrol along with this new lieutenant around some hills. I knew it was the wrong place to be, but that lieutenant thought his Army books were right no matter what.

These 'Paches took out from the trees and come at us. The lieutenant went down right away. We was firin' our pistols and droppin' 'em, but they was on us pretty fast. One of dem bucks got in close and my pistol misfired. He flung his lance; it caught my knee. I come off my hoss and he come off his right on top of me. We fought hard, I tell ya we fought hard. 'Till I got my knife in him. We lost a lot of good men that day. It was a damn fool thang to do."

He shook his head slowly then took another draw from the bottle. "The doc was gonna cut my whole leg off, but the Cap'n made him work on it and not cut it off."

He reached down and rubbed his injured leg as he continued. "Sometimes I wonder if it mighta been better."

Flap Jacks laid back in his bunk then and stared at the ceiling overhead. Deke never asked such questions again.

Carl lived in the big cabin against the canyon wall. It was the headquarters and the place where meetings were held. Every day the gang would gather at a long table that sat in the middle of the yard. Benches and a few old stumps served as chairs. A fire ring was off to the side with a few other stumps scattered around it. Carl would give assignments and pass any word that would be of importance to the boys.

Otherwise the big cabin was a place to be avoided. Deke heard tell of Carl's temper and no man among them would risk bringing it down upon themselves. The only one who would dare confront or interrupt

Carl Ferguson was Bill Sinclair. Sometimes he did it more as a show of his nearest equality than any particular necessity.

Bill had been Carl's right hand man for many years. They had ridden together and knew each other's secrets and shortcomings better than anyone else. He was a gruff man with no presumptions of tolerance for anything or anybody. His concern was making money and taking what he wanted from whomever appeared to be the weakest.

He was a man born of a hard life, who never learned to read or write much beyond the third grade, although Carl had helped him with that some, as much as Bill would let him. He was big and calloused; his beard was stained with tobacco juice. He showed no mercy to those who had been his victims or enemies and thought nothing of swinging one of his club like fists against anyone who got in his way or failed to follow his directions. He was loud, boisterous, and an obnoxious braggart; he bullied those of lesser size and loathed those of greater accomplishment.

As the gang settled into the ranch they were busy putting everything back in order.

They stowed gear and made sure the stock they brought back was turned out in a wide pasture. The unbranded stock and weaned calves were cut out and pushed into one larger herd while the marked stock was pushed into a separate pasture higher up and farther away from the others. They would gather them again shortly and deliver them to buyers who were ready to make shady deals. It was a dangerous business for both sides, but the extra profit it represented coaxed many a man into betraying his own code of ethics.

Flap Jacks and Deke got busy setting up the ranch kitchen as soon as they arrived.

"Betta hurry and brang that food in boy, these fella's is gonna be mighty hungry by nightfall, an' I don't wanna hear 'em belly achin'"

Deke did as he was instructed and kept busy. He was learning fast that he didn't much like kitchen work, but he liked Flap Jacks and was at least glad to have a place and do his part. There wasn't much time, so they threw together what was at hand. Deke was amazed at how quickly the man could move about. His stiffened leg thumping along the ground. He conjured a great meal, enough to feed an army out of what seemed like nothing but cans and smoked beef.

When they were done Flap Jacks pointed at an old cow bell that hung from a rafter in the covered eating area. "Give that thang a big rattle and les' git this bunch fed so's we can get finished up."

When he rang the bell the boys came running, many pushing and shoving to get their plates and get in line as the two spooned up the food.

Slate came through and grinned at Deke, "How's he fillin out?" He asked. Flap Jacks answered for him. "Dis boy's about to eat us out'a house and home. I don't know if we ought'n throw 'im back befo he leaves the rest of us to starve!" The men all laughed at the joke, Deke had to grin in response.

Bill Sinclair shoved his way through the line and thrust his plate out. Flap Jacks' grin faded, and a dark look overtook his features he eyed Bill disdainfully and Bill sneered back in return. "Pile it up, boy!" Deke stood by and watched the exchange, his own contempt for the big man growing in response.

Flap Jacks spooned up only a dab of spuds and splatted it onto Bill's plate. The place grew very quiet. Bill glanced left and right then dropped the plate and grabbed the cook by his collar pulling him half way over the table. He drew his fist back, "I don't take that from no gimp nig...." his words trailed off when the long silver blade laid itself firmly against his throat just under his beard.

Bill froze in place, but still held the man's collar. Flap Jacks' voice was steady, almost a whisper as he seethed his words through gritted teeth glaring into Bill shocked eyes.

"Bill, one a dees days I'm'a gonna cut yo throat, an' when I do, I'm'a gonna cut it deep and slow so you will die lookin' at me jus' like you are right now."

Bill released him then, glaring hatefully. He turned abruptly and shoved his way out but stopped and spun on his heel. "We'll even up, boy!" With that, Bill turned again and walked out. Flap Jacks did not reply but slid the long knife back into its sheath. He picked up the spoon and grinned at the boys still in line. "Wa'll come on. Ya'll didn't lose yo' appetite did ya?"

The place came alive again and the boys shuffled on through. The food was delicious and plentiful for being camp fare. Some of the boys made complaints in jest, but all ate their fill and filed over to wash their plates and utensils in the buckets of hot water that were set aside for that purpose. Deke was rolling up his sleeves to begin scrubbing the pots when Flap Jacks handed him a plate piled high with food. "Take dis upta da big cabin for Carl. He generally takes his meals there." Flap Jacks handed him a second plate piled as high as the first, "And take dis one to Bill, da dirty sumbitch still gotta eat."

Deke carried the food toward the cabin when he saw Bill Sinclair setting on a log sharpening his knife. He said not a word but laid the plate beside him and continued on. Bill spat angrily in the dirt between his toes but picked up the plate and ate hungrily.

There was lamp light in the window of the cabin when Deke stepped up on the porch and knocked on the door. "Yeah!" came the reply from within.

Carl sat at a rough hewn table. He wore a pair of spectacles and he studied some papers that lay before him. He glanced up and saw Deke standing there. He doffed the glasses and laid them down beside him. "Well, how are ya fittin" in?" He asked.

Deke sat the plate on the table before him. "I like it here." He replied.

Carl drew the plate to him and began to eat. He motioned a chair and told him to sit.

Deke took the chair and looked about. The cabin was neat and tidy. There was furniture, made the same as the table. It was rough but sturdy, most made from branches and limbs, smoothed and varnished. They were probably made from the same trees that made up the cabin itself, they were covered with Indian blankets. The colors and patterns served to brighten the room and made it appear larger than it was.

There was a stone fireplace. Rifles leaned in every corner and there was a pistol on every ledge. A painting of a plump, half-naked woman hung on one wall, a cougar skin hung on another and a pair of large antlers hung from a third.

There were two doors, both closed, that led to other rooms that Deke guessed were bedrooms or storage rooms. There was a small nook on one side that held a water pump, a small stove and a counter for preparing meals. His eyes kept returning to the lewd painting causing him to struggle with his conscience.

Deke forced his attention back to the table before him. He noticed then a small ring. He looked at it intently until Carl caught his gaze. "That was your mother's." Carl stated.

Deke suddenly turned cold. Carl picked up the ring and held it up to the light.

"This here ring was also worn by my own mother." He said. Deke had no idea how to reply. Carl looked at him, studying his expression. The boy looked away and Carl decided to pursue the subject no further.

Carl laid the ring back down and finished his supper. He sat back then and rolled a cigarette. "What do ya think of our operation here?" He asked.

Deke shrugged his shoulders. "Most of the boys are okay, I don't like that Bill Sinclair fella though."

Carl laughed and leaned forward, "Nobody likes Bill Sinclair," He said, "But he's a good man to ride with, he's mean as hell though so you steer clear of him, you understand?"

Deke had already made his mind up that he wasn't steering clear of any man any longer, but he nodded to the order in the affirmative.

"Here pretty soon we're gonna gather up that stock and get 'em sold. Then we'll lay back for a while."

"It's quite a place ya got here." Deke replied.

Carl nodded and leaned back. "This here place is just right for this outfit. Here in these parts folks believe that we're a respectable ranchin' operation, legitimate as can be. We don't do no raidin' or 'other' work anywhere near here. The marshal turns an eye away as long as we stay peaceable in his territory and he gets his cut of the profits. Law'n don't pay real good I guess. All our other business is kept real quiet. Most of the folks we do business with are just as concerned for their reputations and necks as we are."

Deke nodded in understanding. Carl eyed him for a long moment, enough to make him uneasy.

"I don't know just yet what I'm gonna do with you."

The statement came as a surprise. "What do you mean?" Deke asked.

"I mean I don't think you oughta stay here and live this kind of life. What would you think about going to a school somewhere? Maybe in Denver or something?"

Deke was put off by the question. He stood up and glared. "There ain't no way in hell I'm going to any damn school in Denver or anywhere else!"

Carl leaned back, "Now hold on there. Your mother would not have wanted you to be here, she would have wanted you to get a better life and...."

"I ain't going to no school! If you don't want me here I'll go somewhere else. It don't matter to me either way!"

Carl's brow furrowed as he eyed the youngster. "Alright, I was just thinkin' about your ma and what..." Deke interrupted with a final statement.

"She's dead."

Carl paused, shifting his jaw. He studied the boy for a moment. "Yup, she sure is."

Carl handed the empty plate back to Deke and nodded toward the door.

He stepped down off the porch his temper flaring as he strode deliberately away.

Bill Sinclair hollered at him as he passed. "Hold up there." Deke stopped in his tracks. Bill rudely dropped his own plate on top of the one Deke carried. He sucked his teeth and poked a toothpick in his mouth as he glared at the boy and turned away.

Fury welled up inside Deke. He was about to go after Bill when Bobby stepped in front of him. "Don't do it." He said.

Bobby saw the anger in Deke's eyes, "There's better ways a gettin' even with the likes of Bill. Drop that stuff off and follow me. I'll show ya."

Deke slipped into the mess tent and quickly, quietly laid the dishes down and slipped back out.

The two went to the tack shed next to the corral and located Bill's saddle. Bobby took the left stirrup and unfastened the catch, loosening the leather strap that held it in place. "Now old Bill will fall on his fat ass when he goes to mount up in the mornin'. It oughta be a hoot!" Bobby was grinning wide, his face full of mischief. Deke chuckled in return and the two hightailed it out and slunk away.

Bobby retired to the bunkhouse, Deke hot footed it back to the kitchen and got busy on the wash bucket. He plunged his arms into the soapy water, scrubbing a pot as if he would rub right through it, a hint of a grin picking at the corners of his mouth. Flap Jacks stopped his own work for minute and stared quizzically. "What's got into you boy?" Deke flushed and buried his chin into his shoulder for moment.

"Nothin" He replied innocently.

The next day the men rounded up their horses and prepared to gather the stolen stock. Bill was gruff and pushy as always as he saddled up his mount. He yanked hard on the cinch and fastened his saddlebags on. He spat a long stream of tobacco juice, placed his foot in the stirrup, his left hand on the pommel and heaved himself up. The stirrup strap came unfurled from around the brace and Bill fell in a heap on the ground!

The fall caused his horse to jump sideways further aggravating his situation. The boys all broke into laughter at Bill's plight. Some doubled over and jeered at the big man who was picking himself up, angrily pounding the dust off himself.

Deke sat aboard the Bay gelding and Bobby was on his mustang. The two looked at each other wide eyed and laughed louder than the rest. Bill picked up on the two youngster's excessive amusement. He stepped toward them, his jaw set rigidly.

"You two little whelps is about to get busted in half!" He growled. Deke and Bobby spurred their mounts away laughing at the big man's irritation. Bill picked up a large stick and hurled it after them then glared at the rest of the men as he stepped back to tend his stirrup. Bill Sinclair was a hard man to get along with on an average day. That day was going to be even harder. It was worth it.

As they rode past the chow line, Flap Jacks looked on and held up his hand. "Hey, boy! Don't ya go getting' used to all dat easy work, you still gotta tend the pots an' pans when ya git back!"

Deke frowned, but waved in return. He was glad to be out doing man's work though he knew his stint as kitchen help was far from over.

The stock was gathered and pointed down the trail. Carl, Bill, Cotton Joe and another man, Heck Braden, headed them down the trail; leaving Slate to look after the operation at home.

After the herd had left, two other men rode in. Shelby Johnson and Johnny Smith were two hired hands. Southerners turned cow punchers who sought an easier way of making a living than riding endless hours nursing another man's cattle.

They were shabby and dusty. They had not been with the outfit long and hadn't quite fit in as yet. They tended to stay to themselves more often than not. Slate walked up to the two as they were unsaddling their horses. "Where ya'll been to?" He asked laying a hand on the rump of one of the horses.

"Aw, we just been out, ridin' the trails and seein' the sights." Shelby replied with a grin, showing his crooked, yellow and chipped teeth.

Johnny was tall and lanky, with black oily hair. He laughed at his friend's explanation as he loosened the rigging on his saddle.

Slate patted the horse next to him. "Looks like ya been ridin' kinda hard. These hosses are lathered up pretty good."

Shelby didn't look away from what he was doing. "Aw, these hosses are just fine. Good for 'em to get a little sweaty."

Slate nodded and walked away rubbing his chin.

The day went along quietly. Deke helped Flap Jacks get the field kitchen squared away and lent a hand to Bobby, who was mending some bridles and oiling his saddle. Bobby wore a holster that had silver beads around the edge and a concho made from a hammered silver dollar. Deke admired the rig. Bobby unswung it from around his hips and handed it over. "Here, try it on."

Taking the holster and belt in hand, Deke felt the heft of the pistol carried within.

He held it up and turned it around looking at the fancy leather work. He strapped it around himself needing another notch or two than the well-worn one Bobby normally used.

Bobby eyed him with a thoughtful stare. "Now that looks like it fits ya pretty good. It set me back a pretty penny. Maybe we can find one for you when we get the chance. Meantime there's a couple of old rigs in the tack shed. Maybe one of those will do ya for now."

Deke unfastened the gun belt and handed it back. "I'm gonna get me one of these!" He said.

The two rustled around a pile of leather gear that had been stowed away. They pulled out three gun belts and studied them. One was much too large for Deke's narrow frame. The other two fit but needed some repair. He finally settled on the plainest of the two but took the fancy buckle from the large one and affixed to the one he took. He fetched his old Colt, strapped on the belt and thrust the gun into the holster.

Bobby stepped back eyeing him again as he did the first time. "Yep. That oughta do ya! You look like a regular pistolero."

Deke felt the weight of the gun on his hip, hitched it up, and settled it back in place. He drew the old revolver back and forth a couple of times. The gun was too big and long-barreled, and the boy needed some practice. Bobby said as much. "When Cotton gets back we'll get with him and he can show ya how to shuck that thing and make it count." He added.

Deke grinned and nodded in reply.

The men sat around the big table. Bill leaned back absentmindedly prodding at a sliver in the heel of his hand with the point of a pocket knife. Shelby, Johnny and Heck Braden tossed cards in a casual game of poker. Bobby and Deke sat across from each other cleaning their guns and talking. Carl strode up to the group a cup of coffee in his hand. He circled the table thoughtfully. Placing the cup on the rough table top he looked at Bill. "Bill." He said in a louder than normal voice.

"What's the rule on free lancin' in these parts?"

Bill looked up at the big man quizzically. "There ain't to be no free lancin'." He replied.

Carl nodded and walked around to where Shelby and Johnny sat. The two exchanged a nervous glance. "Anybody know anything about a couple folks that was held up on the town road a few days ago?"

His eyes focused on the two before him. Shelby's hand started to quiver, Johnny's eyes grew a little wider. Shelby stood up. "Now listen, Carl, we was just tryin' to have a little fun and make a few extra dollars is all. Nobody got hurt and them pilgrims swore they wouldn't tell nobody." Johnny nodded earnestly. His complexion had turned pale.

Carl eyed the man scornfully. "Got all of two dollars and a half did ya?" The two exchanged another nervous glance. Shelby shrugged his shoulders. "We didn't count it. We didn't figure anyone would find out."

Bill had sat up straight by now his hand moving to a place just above his gun.

Some of the others had begun to move away.

Carl took a deep breath. "I make it my business to 'find out'." He replied. His eyes were angry and mean as he glowered at Shelby. He asked again without moving his stare. "Bill, what's the rule on free lancin'?"

"There ain't to be none." Bill growled in reply, his gaze fastened pointedly on the two miscreants. Shelby glanced about, fear rose up in him.

"Now Carl, go easy I don't want to have to..."

Shelby grabbed for his gun. Carl shucked his and fired before the other man's hand had barely touched the weapon at his side. The bullet smoked dead-center through his chest, smashing the man's heart as it crashed through his body. Shelby staggered back and crumpled to the ground.

Johnny leapt to his feet holding his hands up frantically. "I swear, Carl, we didn't mean nothin'! I swear it won't happen again!"

Carl shifted his glare to Johnny. "I figure you ain't smart enough to have come up with the idea on your own. So, I'll tell ya what we're gonna do. You drop that gun belt and empty your pockets, get that broken down old sorrel, and ride out of here right now. You take the clothes on your back and you'd better get to movin' before I change my mind and send your sorry ass outta here buck naked!

Johnny's shoulders dropped. "You can't send me outta here with no gun or nothin',

I won't last a week without my gear!" He argued.

Carl pointed his gun at Johnny's face and drew back the hammer sneering at the man. "You won't last two more minutes if you stand here jawin'. Now do as I said!"

Johnny unbuckled his gun belt and swung it off, laying it down before him. He dug into his pockets and emptied the contents onto the table. A few dollar bills, some coins, a pocket knife, a few strands of rawhide string, and an old rabbits' foot was all he had.

Heck Braden, grim faced and scowling, had brought the old sorrel and handed it over. The animal wore only a rope halter. Johnny took the horse, his eyes shifting back and forth.

Bill Sinclair stood and glowered at him. "Pick up your friend there and take him with you." Johnny looked at him as if he were crazy. "Take him with... why, Bill, he's dead!"

"I know he's dead, you idiot! Otherwise I'd be talkin' to him! Now pick the bastard up and take him with you! And I'd better not find his stinkin' corpse anywhere around here!"

Johnny guided the horse over to where Shelby lay. "Clean out his pockets and unstrap his rig." Bill instructed.

Johnny leaned to the task. He unbuckled the dead man's gun belt and shuffled in his pockets. He withdrew the contents and placed them angrily on the table next to his own. He struggled beneath the weight of his dead partner, trying to lift and drag the body. No one made a move to help. He finally heaved the body over the horse's rump. He was smeared with his friend's blood when he climbed astride and prodded the animal to move out. His feet dangled awkwardly at the horse's side as he shambled away.

"Shoulda just went ahead and shot that sumbitch." Bill spat looking angrily after him.

Carl opened the cylinder on his Colt and thumbed out the spent shell. He flicked it away and withdrew another round from his belt and jammed it in place. He spun the cylinder closed and thrust the weapon into its holster. He turned to walk away,

"Divvy that stuff up between ya." He said, motioning at the piles left from the pockets of the dead and the banished.

Bill snatched up the paper bills, the rest went here and there. Deke plucked up the rabbit's foot and rubbed the fur between his fingers. Heck grabbed a pocket knife that had been pulled from Shelby's pockets and picking up the one that was Johnny's, tossed it over to Deke.

Deke took the knife gladly. but was eyeing the gun rig that had been Shelby's. Bobby picked it up and held it at arm's length. "Oughta be good as new, Shelby never was much of a gun hand. He was always more show than go." Bill pulled the rig from his hand and sat it on the table.

"Their guns and gear will be auctioned tonight after supper." Bill said.

Deke looked surprised. Bobby explained. "Anytime we lose a man; whether he gets arrested, killed or run off, we have an auction of their guns and gear. The money either goes to the man's family if he has one or into the coffers for expenses. Sometimes when we get to town Carl will put it on the bar and we'll all drink on the dead man's dime." He finished that last sentence with a mischievous grin hiking his eyebrows for punctuation.

Slate and Heck gathered the departed men's gear from the bunkhouse and tack room. After supper it was all laid out on the wide table. The men gathered around as Carl stepped up on a stump. He passed a couple of bottles into the little crowd and spoke.

"Boys, you know the deal here so we ain't gonna go into any explanations. Shelby and Johnny decided to leave us and left behind their valuables. We'll open the bidding on this here pile of clothes that was

Shelby's. Don't worry, he took the soiled ones with him." His statement brought a chorus of laughter.

"Okay, now, what am I bid for this here pile of clothes?"

The gang was silent.

"Now come on boys, there's some decent duds in there. How about four bits?"

A man raised his arm. "Sold!" Carl exclaimed.

The bidding went along through all the bequeathed and abandoned belongings.

Saddles and tack went after the clothing and personal items then Carl held up Johnny's gun belt.

"Here ya go." He said. "A nice, not-too-worn-out rig with a Schofield."

The bidding went to seven dollars. Heck Braden was partial to Schofields and took ownership of the gun and holster.

Deke had been silent throughout the proceedings. Several items had passed that caught his interest, but Shelby's gun rig held his attention. He elbowed Bobby when Carl picked it up.

"Now here is a..." Carl's words were cut short when Deke blurted out "Five dollars!"

The crowd snickered at the youth's exuberance

Carl paused only a moment, amused as well. "I got five dollars, who'll go six?"

Bill Sinclair stepped in and raised his hand.

Deke felt like he'd been slapped. His face turned redder than it already was.

"Seven dollars!" He said.

"Seven and two bits!" Bill spat.

Deke took a deep breath. He was getting nervous, knowing he had only nine dollars to his name. He figured Bill knew that too.

"Eight dollars!"

"Eight and two bits!

Deke eyed Bill angrily, the big man returned his glare with smug authority.

Deke felt a nudge at his side. Cotton Joe stood behind his shoulder and said in a low voice, "Keep goin', I'll stand ya. Don't let that prick win."

Deke's jaw was clenched in determination. "I got nine dollars!"

Bill smirked. "Nine dollars and two bits!"

Cotton Joe nudged him, "Go ahead." He whispered.

Deke's head was spinning. "N-Nine dollars and f-four bits!"

Carl looked back and forth between the two, amused at the spectacle.

Bill placed his hands on his hips, his eyes narrowed, looking straight at his opponent.

"Ten dollars!"

Deke felt the nudge again. "Ten dollars and two bits!"

"You ain't got ten dollars and two bits boy!" Bill accused.

Cotton nudged him again "Go twelve, don't worry, I'll stand ya."

"Deke stepped forward in a surge of confidence. "I got twelve dollars for that there rig!"

Bill sneered at him. "Bah! It's all yours, just don't shoot your damn fool foot off!"

He raised his hands and stepped away. Cotton Joe stuffed three dollars in Deke's hand. "Go buy your gun." He said.

Deke took the get up and eyed it with interest. It wasn't as decked out as Bobby's, but it was well made and not near as plain and worn as the old rig he'd rescued from the tack shed. The gun was a Colt

Peacemaker. It needed cleaning, but it was a weapon that outclassed the old Navy he'd brought with him. Still, he replaced the buckle with the one from the old belt and proudly took possession of the dead man's gun. As he strapped the rig on he looked over at Cotton Joe. "Thanks Cotton, I'll pay ya back just as soon as I get it to give ya."

Cotton smiled at him and waved him off, nodding approvingly at the set of the weapon on Deke's hips. "Don't worry 'bout it. It was worth three dollars to see old Bill get flustered. Tell ya what, come on down to the holler tomorrow after your chores are done and I'll show ya how to use that thing."

Deke grinned eagerly, "Alright, can Bobby come along?" Cotton eyed both, "Sure, why not. Bring a couple of boxes of cartridges."

Cotton walked away. He felt Bill Sinclair's scowl on his back as he took a seat at the table and helped himself to a big gulp from the bottle. He smiled.

Deke rubbed the oiled barrel of the old Colt Navy, the pistol that had delivered him to where he was. A memory of his mother and the kitchen drawer flashed across his mind. Flames rolled and twisted in fierce columns as his mind replayed the significance of the old weapon. He saw the last flutter of his mother's blue eyes once again, heard the gunshots, and saw the sprawling body of his father. He felt the hatred for the man and a lonesome ache for the loss of his mother.

He rolled the gun up in a cloth and stowed it away. "For varmints and rabid dogs and other critters that sneak around in the middle of the night." He whispered.

Chores were done by ten o'clock the next day. Loud reports came from the hollow down by the creek.

Cotton Joe, Deke and Bobby were practicing their marksmanship and gun-handling.

Cotton was the fastest among the gang. His aim was unerring, and his skill was deadly. He set some cans on a rail and stood back.

"Now do as I showed ya." He said. "Focus your eye on where you want the bullet to hit, draw smoothly, until you're pointin' at that spot, and squeeze the trigger."

The two younger men did as instructed. Bobby had more experience and was a fair shake, but by no means a polished gunman. He could yank his pistol with respectable speed, but he rarely got his first bullet on target. Deke on the other hand was a fast learner. He fumbled at first, but he gained skill quickly. Both young men pulled their pistols and fired. Both cans sat unscathed in their places.

Cotton's shoulders slumped, and he rolled his eyes. "Let me show ya again. Now remember; slow is smooth, and smooth is fast." Deke and Bobby exchanged puzzled glances.

He stood between the two. Cotton shucked his pistol, the first round fired as the gun leveled, the second less than a heartbeat later. Both cans flew from their perches' new holes punched right next to the ones from earlier. Even slowing his movements down for the sake of instruction, he was faster than most men at their best.

Deke watched intently. He stepped up to the line, an old branch laid across the ground. "I think I got it."

His hand moved in a fluid motion, withdrawing the Colt as his thumb rocked back the hammer. The gun swung up and erupted just as it stopped in its arc. The bullet pierced the old can right above Cotton's shot. He swung the weapon smoothly to the next can with the same result. He dropped the gun back in its holster, thrust his shoulders back and grinned. "How's that?"

Cotton reached a hand up pushing the brim of his hat with an index finger. "Well, I'll be darned! That's good shootin'. I can tell you got some of old Carl's blood in ya!" He exclaimed.

Bobby stepped up and took his turn. He struck the first can at its side sending it spinning away. He missed the second one, splintering the wood beneath it.

They continued for an hour more. Both improved but Deke's ability seemed to come as natural to him as walking. By the time they called it quits, his movements were a blur and his bullets struck dead on.

As they walked back to the ranch Bobby joshed his friend. "If we ever get in a gun scrape, be a pal and make sure I don't get shot."

When they reached the bunkhouse they saw Heck, shaved and combed, buttoning on a clean shirt.

"You gettin' married or somethin'?" Bobby asked.

"Didn't you two gun-slingers get the word? We're goin' to town, Carl says it's high time to cut the wolf loose and I couldn't agree with the old boy more!"

Bobby turned to his friend. "Better get cleaned up Deke... we're gonna do some howlin'!"

CHAPTER THREE

Carl sat at the long table and parceled out the proceeds from the recent sale of the rustled stock and disposition of other procured articles.

He handed Deke his share and smiled. "You're not a full draw yet, but this oughta do ya for a time." Deke took the money happily. He drew out three dollars and went off to find Cotton Joe.

Carl called after him stopping him in his steps. "Hey, Deke. How about saddling up my horse for me?" Deke nodded then started to walk again when Carl called after him again. "Oh, and Deke..." The boy turned around and looked. "Leave the stirrups alone."

Deke grinned in reply, "Yes, Sir", as Bobby stifled a laugh.

The gang drew up on the knoll just out of town. The men sat their horses while Flap Jacks drove the buckboard. Carl addressed the bunch, cautioning every man to stay out of trouble.

"Me, Bill, Cotton, and Slate will go heeled. Flap Jacks keep your scatter gun and rifle loaded, but outta sight in the wagon. The rest of ya roll up them rigs, stuff 'em in your saddle bags. We don't want no gun trouble."

The men did as instructed, though a couple grumbled about it.

They rode in as the sun was setting. Cotton, Deke, and Bobby rode abreast as they ambled into town. Bill said not a word but trotted his mount ahead and continued as though he would ride clean through the town and never stop.

A two story building was on their left. It was a fancy place with white pillars and gold painted trim. Red curtains decorated the windows. A couple of women lounged on the wide veranda, a few more leaned over the rail of the upper balcony. Their ample breasts all but bare. They called out to the passersby.

The three gawked at the ladies' lewd display. Cotton's eye was fastened on a dark haired, slender woman, who swayed seductively and raised a long index finger motioning him to her. He nearly turned his mount but forced his gaze ahead. All three were captivated but shifted their focus on the hotel restaurant ahead. Cotton nervously cleared his throat.

"We'll, ah, get some grub there first boys and then...."

Deke and Bobby simply nodded.

They sat at a cloth covered table and ordered steaks. The lady who took their orders was tall and heavy. Her hair was pulled back in a severe bun. She was a burly woman with large man-like hands and the personality of burlap. Any trace of a smile had long been absent from her stern features.

She warned them to not rake their spurs against the furniture. It was a caution that all took very seriously.

Cotton finished first and stepped outside to take a chair. He rolled a smoke and waited for the others. When Bobby and Deke stepped out Cotton rose from his chair and stretched. "We was gonna go down to the saloon." Bobby said, "You comin' along?"

Cotton took a last drag of his smoke and flipped the butt into the street. His face turned to the parlor they passed earlier. "Maybe I'll meet ya there later. I got some other business to tend to." He said with a wink.

Bobby elbowed him, "Ah c'mon, they got girls at the saloon…" He implored.

Cotton shook his head slowly. "Not like that, they don't. See you fella's later."

Cotton Joe stepped off the porch and sauntered toward the dark haired beauty at the end of the street.

Bobby and Deke stepped into the saloon. It wasn't crowded but it was fairly busy.

They leaned against the bar. Deke's eyes swept the room. He'd never been inside a saloon before and he was full of anticipation.

The bartender was a jovial man. He was white haired with white sideburns that came to the edge of his jaw. A wide mustache connected the two in the center. He grinned at the newcomers then eyed Deke suspiciously. Deke returned the man's stare with confidence and pulled a hand full of dollars from his pocket. The bartender's friendly grin returned rapidly. "What'll you two punchers want?" He asked.

Bobby flipped his thumb back and forth between his companion and himself.

"How 'bout a couple of cold beers."

The bartender nodded, swept up two glass mugs in his hands and turned toward the draught.

When he sat the beers down before the two he gave Deke another cautionary glance. "Now you take it easy in here, son, I can see you got the devil in your eye."

The statement caught Deke by surprise and made him uneasy, he simply nodded in return. He felt good and didn't want the mood spoiled.

The bartender caught the attention of a saloon girl and motioned her toward them.

She strode over picking up one of her associates along the way. The bartender winked at them and smiled, raising his eyebrows.

Each of the girls sidled up between the two. One, a slight built blonde, with green eyes and porcelain complexion, took a liking to Deke. She ran her long fingers through his hair and gently pinched his cheek. "Why, honey, you're as green as grass." She exclaimed.

Deke's face blushed bright red.

Bobby laid his arm around the brunette at his side and ordered drinks for the girls.

"I don't reckon my friend here has a lot of experience, but I'll bet he'll make up for it in determination." He grinned.

By the time he'd finished his beer Deke was completely under the dove's spell. She whispered something in his ear and kissed him ever so lightly on the lips. Deke nodded in hurried agreement. She took him by the hand and led him toward the stairs. Bobby gulped his own beer. "Last one in's a rotten egg!" He hollered as he slammed down the mug, took the hand of his own girl and followed suit.

When they returned from the upstairs rooms, they took a couple of chairs close by the bar. Bobby wondered if the grin on Deke's face was going to be permanent. The lad was starry eyed and flushed. They ordered more beer.

The others had come in and were taking their places as well.

Carl and Slate took a table in the back corner. The Marshal, a large, but droop shouldered man, grown wide in the middle, walked in only a few minutes later. He raked a chair across from them, slouched into it and propped a foot up. Deke watched them intently, trying to pick up on the conversation.

"How's it going, Randy?" Carl said pouring a half glass of whiskey and sliding it over to him.

The marshal took the glass and nodded. "Good and quiet for the most part." He took a sip and sat the glass down. "How 'bout you?"

Carl leaned back and smiled. "Can't complain." As he leaned back he made sure that the envelope he carried was visible from within his coat pocket. He took note of the law man's interest.

The Marshal made idle chat then mentioned something that got Carl's interest up. "I got a boy over at my jail says he knows you."

Carl's smile faded.

"Say's if we don't hang him he'll give the court all the information they need to round up one of the worst outlaw gangs in the territory." The Marshal spoke as if discussing the weather.

Carl leaned back trading cautionary glances with Slate. "That a fact?"

"Yep, says he knows a lot that the law would like to know.

"You say this fella is in your jail?"

"Sure enough. I caught him trying to steal a horse out of the livery a few days ago."

The conversation paused, Carl knew that the lawman was leading up to something and decided to let him pick the trail.

The Marshal emptied his glass and held it over for a refill.

"I checked all my notices and bills but couldn't find one on this fella. I'm sure he's wanted somewhere though. There's gotta be some kind of reward offered on him."

The Marshal stalled for a moment then tapped his finger on the table. "Yep, I'm sure he's wanted somewhere."

Carl nodded, the gist of the conversation was becoming clear.

"How much you figure that fellas worth?" He asked.

"Oh, hell, I don't know, trouble makers like that... I'd bet a month's pay there's somebody'd like to get a hold of him."

Carl leaned forward eyeing the man closely. "How much is a month's pay?"

The Marshal grinned.

When they entered the jail, Carl and Slate were not surprised to see Johnny Smith.

Johnny leaped to his feet. "You got 'em, Marshal!" He exclaimed. The group stood silent watching the man behind the bars pace back and forth. Johnny's exalted demeanor angered Slate.

Johnny glared at Carl and Slate. "I got the law on my side and I'm gonna get out scott-free 'cause I'm gonna tell 'em all they want to know about you and your outfit. You're all gonna hang and I'm gonna watch. Probably even make some money off the deal!"

Johnny strutted and giggled, taunting the men who stared back at him. He pointed a finger at Slate, "I could outgun you, Slate! Always wanted to. I'd shoot you full of holes and pistol whip what was left! Now I'm just gonna watch you stretch a rope!" He pranced around clucking like a strutting rooster. Slate's eyes narrowed.

His face expressionless, Carl reached in his coat, withdrew the envelope, a month's pay thicker, and handed it to the Marshal.

Johnny looked back and forth at them, confused. His face registered shocked surprise, then terror when the Marshal took the key ring from his belt and handed it to Carl. "I don't care what you do with him, just do it far from here."

Johnny screamed and curled up in the corner on top of the bunk as the men entered the cell. Slate's gun came down savagely on top of his head.

Deke watched as the Marshal, Carl and Slate walked from the saloon. His curiosity was up and after a while he went to investigate. He saw the back door of the law office open and a slant of light shine on the steps. Carl looked out and saw him there. He shook his head and cursed then told him to go get their horses. Deke ran to the hitch rail and retrieved the mounts as well as his own.

Slate was holding an unconscious Johnny Smith by the collar. "Gimme a hand."

The two heaved Smith's frame across the rump of Slate's horse. Carl took his reins and motioned to the two. I'll stay here, back over to the saloon. You two take care of this."

Slate nodded and boarded the saddle, Deke followed as they rode toward the prairie. Slate explained the story as they went. There was no need to discuss the outcome. Deke reached in his saddle bag and pulled his gun belt out an' strapped it on.

After a while Johnny began to rustle about. They were a few miles out before they came to a deep arroyo and were far enough and downwind of the town to not worry about sound traveling to unwanted ears. Slate halted his mount and dumped Johnny roughly to the ground. The man staggered to his feet holding his head.

"Wh-What's goin' on?" He asked weakly.

Slate glared at him, his hand resting on the butt of his pistol. "You had a chance boy! You shoulda took it."

Johnny looked up at the two. He raised his hands in front of him.

"Ah, C'mon Slate, I- I was just joshin' I wasn't about tell 'em anything. I was just trying to stall 'em long enough to figure out a way to escape!"

He paced to and fro as he talked. Seeing no sign in Slate's cold eyes, he shifted his plea to the younger face on the bay.

"Hey boy, Deke, right? Y- you know me. W-we're pals, right? Be a pard and talk this fella into lettin' me go. Say, ain't them Shelby's guns?" He noticed. A grim recognition shadowed his face. He forced an apologetic grin. "Well, old Shelby wasn't much of a gun hand anyhow ya know. They look better on you."

He quickly stepped back to Slate, hopping around like he was standing on hot coals. "Ya'll ain't got nothin to worry about. I'll just skedaddle on outta here and you'll never see me again. I swear!" Still seeing no hint of sympathy, he went back to Deke. "Come on pal, give an old friend a break…"

He placed his hand on Deke's knee pleading for his life. Deke smiled at him then turned to Slate. Slate's face was grim, but he made no other indication. A look of hope flashed across Johnny's face as he looked between the two, then Deke pulled his gun from its holster and shot him between the eyes.

Slate watched him for a moment. Deke calmly opened the cylinder, plucked out the spent cartridge, flicked it away and replaced it with a new one in the same manner in which he'd seen Carl accomplish the same task. He spun the cylinder closed, stuffed the Colt in its holster, and looked over at Slate grinning. The boy was cold, he could see that. Slate decided right then and there that Deke was dangerous, more so than he should have been.

Slate stepped down from his horse and over to where Johnny lay, his dead eyes staring vacantly at the stars above. "Let's toss him over in this gully."

Deke stepped down and grabbed a hold of Johnny's feet. The two carried the dead man to the edge of the arroyo and swung him out and let go. The body hit with a thud.

"I guess that takes care of it." Slate said.

Deke replied with a grin. "Ready to go back?"

Slate shrugged and glared at the body lying in an awkward heap. "I reckon the coyotes and buzzards will clean up the mess."

By the time they were halfway back to town they could here behind them the yips and howls of a coyote pack snarling, tearing, and feeding. Deke turned back in his saddle looking toward the sounds and laughed. Slate spoke over his shoulder,

"Better wrap that iron up and put it back in your saddle bag. Carl ain't gonna want any extra guns dangling around." Deke didn't like it but did as instructed.

They walked back into the saloon. Carl sat with Bobby and Cotton. Slate pulled a chair over and reached for a glass, Deke did the same. Carl's hand came down firmly on the glass as the young man pulled it to him. He shook his head. "Have a beer." Deke met Carl's eyes, the warning was plain and simple and there would be no discussion.

Carl exchanged a glance with Slate. They spoke no words, but the question was understood and answered. Slate made a nod toward to Deke. Carl raised an eyebrow and nodded to the boy. Slate leaned back and studied him contemplatively. Carl raised his glass. "Here's to ya boys!"

The men at the table joined in and they all drank.

"Where's Flap Jacks?" Deke asked.

Cotton snorted a heavy laugh. "He's down at the parlor. They got a nice creole girl there. She sure is pretty. That's where he'll spend all his time. I'm startin' to wonder if them two ain't in love." He said the last word with a flourish.

The men all cheered. "To Flap Jacks and his girl!" they toasted.

Carl pulled a wad of cash and a handful of coins from his pocket. He motioned the bartender over. He handed the money to him. "Drinks until it's gone." The bartender's face lit up "Yes, Sir!" He went behind the bar and rang a bell. Carl smiled at the others "Looks like Shelby and Johnny are buyin' drinks boys!" The saloon girls moved in closer to the men and plied their wares earnestly.

The blonde girl wrapped an arm around Deke and gazed seductively into his eyes. He handed her a glass, the blush on his face growing darker. Bobby pulled the brunette onto his lap and winked mischievously at his friend.

Cotton Joe leaned back in his chair a cigarette hung from his lip as he idly twirled a silver dollar between his fingers working it back and forth from his little finger to his thumb. Deke watched, intrigued with the display of dexterity. He drew out a silver dollar and attempted the same trick. He fumbled and dropped the heavy coin a few times, but on the fourth try had it moving along across his fingers nearly as smoothly as Cottons. Cotton laughed and nodded his approval.

Before long Deke was digging in his pockets. He withdrew two dollars. The last he had and taking the blonde saloon girl by the hand retraced their earlier path.

Bobby grinned. "That boy is a terror." Slate raised an eyebrow "You might be right." He answered flatly.

The next morning the men gathered their horses and prepared for the trip back to the home place. Deke's head pounded. Bobby looked across his saddle at him obviously suffering in the same manner.

"I think a rattlesnake pissed in my mouth." He said queasily. Deke nodded in agreement. "I guess we're gonna make it, I don't know about Heck though. He indicated the man heaving over the corral rail. Heck straightened up, but then dashed toward the outhouse. "Guess it's a good thing we didn't get in that whiskey."

Flap Jacks was coming up the street in the buckboard. Beside him sat a slight framed, dark skinned woman holding a bundle in her lap. Everyone eyed the pair with curiosity. Carl walked over when he pulled the wagon to a stop in front of the store. He spoke pleasantly, as if nothing was amiss.

"How ya doin' Flap Jacks?" He queried. He smiled and tipped his hat to the woman sitting next to Flap Jacks. She was younger than Flap Jacks by a good bit. She was plain, but still a very attractive girl, who had skin that was lighter than Flap Jacks'. She had a crooked nose, but also had fine teeth and full lips that smiled kindly. Her hair was covered by a bandana, but the wisps that escaped were dark, curly and soft.

Flap Jacks set the brake and hooked the reins on the dashboard. He looked over at the boss and tilted his head back and forth.

"Doin' fine, Carl. This here is Doralee. She's my wife."

Those that heard were taken aback, they exchanged surprised glances and shrugs.

Carl smiled at the lady and tipped his hat again. "Nice to meet you, Mrs. Johnson, and congratulations."

The woman smiled and nodded in return. There was an awkward pause. Then Carl tapped Flap Jacks on the knee. "I wonder if we might have a word over here for a minute." He said then tipped his hat again at Mrs. Johnson, "It'll just be a minute, ma'am." She nodded her smile fading with worry.

Flap Jacks eased himself down from the wagon and the walked around the corner.

"Now, Carl, I know what you're thankin', but I ain't a young man no more and I'm tired of bein' alone. A man ain't meant to be alone. This gal's a good un and I mean to keep her. She can help me around the place." He paused a minute then looked into Carl's eyes an expression on his face that Carl had never seen before. "She makes my leg not hurt."

Carl listened. True, Flap Jacks was getting a little gray and he knew that while the others had the liberty to dally with the whores in the saloons and the ladies at other places, Flap Jacks was, more often than not, excluded.

"We been together a long time." Carl said. "I never knew you to do anything that wasn't right. She's a right pretty gal." He said, but his tone lowered. "What if one of the boys takes a shine to her or if she was to take a shine to one of them?"

Flap Jacks shook his head. "I don't expect that'll happen, that's why I kilt my first wife and she knows that. No, I don't expect that'll happen. A man like me ain't got a lot of options, Carl. Either she goes, or I stay right here."

Carl remembered the Navajo girl that Flap Jacks mentioned. She was as loose as a pole cat in heat. He had even given her a toss or two himself. He sure wasn't going to admit that to Flap Jacks though. Flap Jacks knew, but never addressed it. He'd never known what had happened to her just that one day she was gone. That was a long time ago.

"I need ya, Flap Jacks. The boys need ya. I reckon if you trust her then she must be a mighty fine woman. Hell, it might make the old camp a better place having Mrs. Johnson around."

Carl grinned and offered his hand. Flap Jacks returned the grin and the two shook firmly, slapping each other's shoulder.

When the two walked back the boys sat on the steps of the store, their horses tied to the rail. Deke and Bobby were talking with Doralee. "She says she can make sweet corn bread and sugar rolls!" Deke exclaimed as they arrived alongside.

Flap Jacks laughed and patted his bride on the hand "I reckon she can make anything sweet!"

"Alright, let's get the supplies loaded up and head out. We got a long day ahead of us." Carl interjected.

Flap Jacks helped Doralee down from the wagon. "You'd might as well start right now. He handed her a long list from his pocket and they went inside. He looked over at Deke. "Boy, I reckon your time as kitchen help is done. We get back you move your gear over to the bunk house." Deke nodded eagerly. "Yes, Sir!" It was good news.

As they loaded the wagon Bill Sinclair walked his horse down the street toward them and swung down from the saddle. His hair was cut, beard trimmed, and he wore a pressed shirt. Heck was feeling a little better than earlier and guffawed at Bill's neat appearance. "Where you been, Sunday school?"

He started to laugh when Bill grabbed him by the collar. He pulled the man close and sneered in his face "None of your business, pup!" He shoved Heck away and glared at him. Heck staggered back, only the rail kept him from falling down. The humor had left his face and he glared back at the big man.

Doralee walked by Bill carrying a box of goods. Bill looked at her and raised his eyebrows. Carl stepped up beside him. "Bill Sinclair meet Mrs. Flap Jacks Johnson." Bill's face went blank. "This outfit is goin' to hell." He huffed. "Guess if we're gonna have a bunch of young'uns we'd just as well have a nanny goat to tend 'em!"

Flap Jacks gave Bill a warning look. His scowl was tangible as he brushed his hand across the big knife that hung at his side.

Doralee saw the anger between the two. She stepped up to Bill holding a large jar of peaches smiling sweetly, her head tilted slightly to the side. "Do you like cobbler?" she asked.

Bill was taken aback. He mumbled a minute, caught off guard by the woman's demeanor. "I make the best peach cobbler. You oughta try it, Mr. Sinclair." Her voice had the sugary julep of a southern accent with a touch of warm-butter-creole cooking. It was very pleasant to the ears of men who were usually without the soft tone of a female voice.

"I- I guess so." He stammered back, completely disarmed. She turned and placed the jar back in the box. "I'm gonna make a peach cobbler for you, Mr. Sinclair."

Bill blinked and suddenly the hint of a smile crossed his face, the appearance of which was as surprising to the rest as the announcement of Flap Jacks marriage.

Flap Jacks elbowed Carl. "I told ya she was a good un!" He grinned.

The crew hustled in and out of the store carrying the supplies and eyeing some of the tack and sundries that were on display. Bobby walked over to Deke and handed him a peppermint stick, one of a dozen he now carried in a little sack.

Deke was staring at a calendar on the wall. "What day is this?" He asked. Bobby studied it and shrugged. "I ain't real sure." Just then the clerk piped in. "It's the twenty-third." He stated flatly.

Deke smiled "Hey, yesterday was my birthday. I'm seventeen now!"

Bobby slapped him on the shoulder, "Happy birthday pard!" he said. "I guess we celebrated right well." Deke nodded and grinned, his mind replaying the comforts of the saloon girl as well as the satisfying recoil of the gun in his hand when he killed Johnny. It was only a second thought and not one that caused him any remorse. "Yep, I guess we did." He replied.

On the ride back, the boys took turns riding by the wagon asking Doralee about cookies and cakes and such. Flap Jacks finally waved them away. "You no-accounts stop pesterin' Mrs. Johnson. She's got no time to be a worryin' about your sweet tooth!"

Doralee smiled, pleased at the attention. She laid her head on Flapjacks' shoulder. She looked contented and her husband beamed proudly.

Carl held his horse until Deke caught up and rode alongside him for a while. He reached in his shirt pocket and pulled out a large silver concho with intricate engraving and handed it over to him.

"What's this for?" Deke asked.

Carl smiled back at him "It's a birthday present, you can string that onto your holster or your belt, or wherever."

Deke held the gift up between himself and the sun, admiring the shine and handy work etched in it. "I ain't never had a birthday present before."

Carl nodded and gave him a confident wink as he spurred his horse on.

After returning to the ranch, Deke quickly gathered up his bedroll and the meager gear he had accumulated and moved to the bunkhouse. As he left, he saw Flapjacks sweep Doralee into his arms and carry her in to the little cabin. Flap Jacks lost his balance on his bad leg but caught himself on the door jamb as he entered. The two were laughing like school kids.

He picked a bunk next to Bobby's and threw his blankets on to it. He withdrew the concho from his pocket, found a leather string and affixed it to his holster. He eyed his handy work and let his fingertips fall to it as the gun hung at his side.

The dinner bell rang and the stampede of boots was all but frantic. Doralee, her hair tied up in a blue bandana, smiled as the boys passed through the line. She nodded sweetly to every "Thank you, ma'am." as she filled their plates.

Bill shuffled in grabbing a plate. Doralee saw him and withdrew a steaming cast iron oven from behind the rough counter. "Mr. Bill...?" she asked, "Would you like your dessert first?" Bill paused, confused by the unaccustomed treatment. "Uh, I don't know." He stammered.

Doralee took his plate from his hand and piled it high. Steam rose from Bill's plate, carrying with it the sweet and delicious fragrance of freshly made peach cobbler. She handed him a fork. He looked at it as if he'd never seen one before. "Go ahead." She urged him. He dug the instrument into the cobbler and placed it carefully in his mouth. Doralee stood smiling, yet nervous. Flap Jacks watched the big man cautiously. Bill's smile was enough to split wood. "Damn, that's good!" He exclaimed. Doralee clapped happily. "I told you I make the best peach cobbler!"

"Yes, ma'am, I'd say you do!" He confirmed. "Now you set right on down and have your fill." She said. The others stared in disbelief. They had just witnessed an old bear get his claws trimmed without a shot fired.

******

Bill Sinclair eyed Carl coolly as Slate explained what had taken place with Johnny Smith. "That boy is cold Carl, he's got a mean streak that'll bust loose one of these days. He bears watchin'." Carl nodded rubbing his chin. "Shoulda just shot that sumbitch in the first place." Bill argued, referring to Johnny.

The three men sat around the table in Carl's cabin discussing the business of the operation when the subject came up. Slate continued. "Johnny got what he needed, but the way that boy shucked his pistol and blew his brains out with no more trouble than swattin' a fly reminds me of some others I've known.

Be careful with him is all I'm sayin'. There might be hell to pay if he busts loose."

Bill interjected, "I still don't know why you brought that boy in here."

Carl's hand dropped to the table and he looked squarely at Bill. "That's my business Bill. Besides, he's shaping up to a pretty good hand. He just needs some polishin' is all."

Bill leaned forward and spoke quietly. "You ever gonna tell him?" Carl sat upright, his face blank, eyes cold. It was a reference to a dark and haunting memory, something that was never to be spoken of. Only the three present knew of that. It was long ago and had taken Bill and Slate a long time to get Carl sobered up and straightened out. It was a chapter Carl wished he could forget.

Slate sat back cautiously, eyeing the exchange between the two. There was a tangible pause. Carl made no reply. Finally Slate dropped his hands on the table breaking the uneasy spell. "Well, I reckon Deke'll shape up just fine. I'll keep an eye on him, Carl." He looked back over at Bill. "Don't go pushin' him, Bill. He's just a pup, but that pup is growin' some mighty big fangs."

******

The months following held just the usual business of a legitimate, growing cattle ranch.

There were branding and gatherings. Some stock was shipped out along with a few of the horses that had grown tired and lame. The boys tended the cattle, fixed and repaired fences and dug a well. They cut hay and laid it up for the winter months, improved stream beds, and cut a canal to fill up a pond.

Deke grew strong in the work and formed up to be a top hand. He, Bobby, and Cotton worked on their gun handling now and then. They were down in the draw with a few of the others practicing their guns when Cotton called him aside.

"Watch Heck there." He motioned with his chin. Heck was fast and accurate. His skill with a gun was comparable to Cotton's. Heck pulled his gun and fired in the space of an eye blink. The old coffee can flew away from its perch punched dead center.

"There. Did ya see that?" Deke looked and shrugged. "See what?" Cotton indicated Heck again. "Watch him when he draws."

Heck repeated the same motion with the same result unaware he was being studied. "I guess I'm just watching Heck shoot a coffee can." Deke replied, with a curious tone.

Cotton nudged him as if he was telling him a secret. "Watch his left elbow."

Heck continued to draw and shoot. The others hollered their approval of his skill. Cotton spoke softly, causing Deke to lean toward him to hear. "Most men, not all mind you, but most have some sort of twitch or motion just before they draw." Deke watched and studied.

Sure enough, Heck's left elbow twitched just as his right arm went for his pistol. Not enough to be noticeable to anyone who wasn't looking for it. But it was there.

"Those are the things ya gotta look for." Cotton explained. A man might be a might faster on the draw, but you can beat him if you know what to look for." The idea took root in Deke's mind and he nodded. He watched the others work their weapons with a different eye now. Cotton continued, "He don't even know he's doing it. If you can see those things first, you don't wait until he goes for his gun, you pull iron at the same time he decides to. It ain't much, but it's enough edge to keep you from getting killed instead of the other guy."

Deke absorbed the information like a sponge. Then thought of his own growing skill. "You notice me doing anything like that?" He asked. Cotton looked at him and smiled. "If I did, I wouldn't tell you."

It was a Sunday afternoon. The sun was setting easily, and a cool breeze played through the canyon. Deke walked toward the bunk house after putting up his horse.

He spent a lot of time with the animal. Picking its hooves and brushing it down. He knew that a man was better off on a horse that he knew and that knew him.

Deke coiled his rope as he passed the field kitchen. Flap Jacks leaned back in a chair his leg propped up on a crate. Doralee sat on another crate and rubbed his injured knee returning his smile coyly.

Deke stepped over and leaned against the porch rail. "How's ya gettin' along?" Flap Jacks asked sleepily. Deke nodded, "Doin' just fine." He watched Doralee's languid arms reaching out gracefully as her long fingers massaged the old soldier's leg.

She smiled politely at him, nodded, but said nothing. Deke watched the two communicate with no spoken words. He suddenly felt awkward, that his presence was an intrusion.

"Boy, I'm glad to see ya, but I thank Mrs. Johnson is growin a might tired and I thank we gonna call it a day." Flap Jacks said with a nod smilin' down at his wife. Doralee blushed, continuing her work. Deke nodded, getting the suggestion and continued his walk. He heard the lady giggle as he left.

The men saw Flap Jacks differently since he got married. Suddenly he became older and wiser in their minds. He had obtained something that all could only wish for. They were happy for him and proud of the couple. Though all were very cautious while in the presence of Mrs. Johnson. One misunderstood word or action could lead a man into the focus of Flap Jacks Johnson's ire; that was no place any man wanted to be.

Carl stood at the head of the table. Bill sat to one side and Slate sat across from him. A map lay between the two.

"There's gonna be freight comin' up from Mexico full of Mexican silver." Carl said pointing toward the south road that led up from the border. "The Army ain't got nothin better to do than to guard that there wagon."

Bill looked over at Slate then up to Carl. "Now what's that got to do with us? We ain't gonna tangle with a company of soldiers."

Carl nodded. "No, we ain't. So, we gotta give 'em more to worry about so's they don't have soldiers guarding that there wagon. That silver is headed to some rancho in California. I don't figure he needs it any more than we do and the government ain't gonna put soldiers on it if they got better things to do."

He indicated the east-west roads that ran north of the border. "There hasn't been much goin' on around here to give the law or the Army much to do. We're gonna change that."

Slate studied the map then the light of an idea illuminated his features. "You figure if we do some raidin' and hell raisin' on these other roads then they'll have to send some men to cover that territory, leavin' less to guard that Mexican silver wagon?"

Carl smiled and nodded. "Divide and conquer. Ain't that what that old Roman said?"

Bill shrugged his reply blankly. "I don't know nothin' about no old Romans, but I get your point."

"What we'll do is send some boys down to these two roads here. We'll hold up stages and raid stations. We'll cause enough trouble to get the law's attention then we'll hold some fellas down south a ways and catch that wagon. If it works out, the guard detail will only be about half of what it should be."

"That's mighty risky, boss." Slate answered.

Bill nodded in agreement.

Carl agreed as well. "Risky for sure, but if we can get a hold of that silver, it'll be worth it."

The men leaned into their conversation eyeing the map. Selecting points for hold ups and hide outs, escape routes and look outs.

Carl eyed the two men before him. "I want you two to pick a few men and head on out. Bill, you take the stations and Slate, you take the coaches. I'll take Cotton and a couple others and head on down toward the border and wait for you there.

We'll make like we're building a herd and speculating for some land. That'll give us a chance to scout the area without too many questions. It'll be about a month before that wagon comes our way. I'll meet ya'll down there. Do what you have to, but don't do no killin' less it's forced on ya."

No further mention of the load of silver was made. The fewer that knew, the better for the overall security of the plan.

That evening Slate picked the men to accompany him. Heck Braden, along with a man named Smitty, and Deke. "You fella's get your gear together and draw some supplies. We'll take two pack horses and that's it, we might be gone a while."

Tracy T. Thurman

CHAPTER FOUR

Smitty was an older man, grizzled and square jawed. He'd been up the river and over the mountain many times. He had worked for the outfit for a few years and was generally a good hand around the ranch, but was especially adept at hold ups, breaking locks and altering brands on cattle. How he stayed ahead of the hangman for so many years was a wonder.

He knew when something big was stirring and it got his interest up. "What are we gonna do, Slate, march through Georgia?" His question challenged Slate's authority.

"We're gonna do what we're told." He said gruffly. The statement and the mode of the delivery grated on Smitty's pride. The two didn't have a very good start to the trip.

As Deke packed his war bag and readied his bed roll, Bobby came up to him and handed him a handful of bandanas. "You might need these. I got plenty from that bunch of clothes I bought that was Johnny's. Don't use the same one twice." He said. Deke took the colorful cloths and picked a red one to tie around his neck, the others he stuffed into his bag. "Thanks, wish you were going with us." He said.

Bobby stuffed his hands in his pockets. "Yeah, I'm goin' somewhere with Bill, Charlie and Thomas." The two he mentioned were not particularly good at anything and were somewhat of a puzzle to him. Deke made an expression of pain in response. "What do you think is going on?"

Bobby shrugged "I don't know, guess we're gonna go out on the hoot-owl trail for a while. I was kind of hoping to stay back here and just do ranch work for a while."

Deke yanked the buckle tight on his bed roll. "Yeah, I'm ready to go raise some hell myself." Bobby laughed. "I figured you might be. Just don't get your head shot off." The two shook hands when they parted. "Good luck to ya." "And you too!"

Slate walked his horse past the rest of the bunch, looking them over coolly. The pack horses were checked and seemed eager to get on the road.

"Deke, you keep an eye out and don't get too grabby with that pistol." He said. He eyed the others, giving them a nod that the same advice applied to them as well.

Bill Sinclair and his bunch left the camp the following day and struck out to the east. Bobby fell on the trail behind the others. He didn't like Bill and was distrustful of the others. He knew, however, that

Bill was a capable, although an overbearing, leader and he put his faith in the big man's experience. He made sure that his gun was well oiled.

Slate's bunch trailed off into the hills that, once crested, would lead them out to the road. Slate was in the lead, then Deke, followed by the first pack horse, then Heck,

Smitty fell in behind the last pack horse and plodded along. He was glad to be away from the ranch and the labor that it required. Heck snatched a chunk from his chewing tobacco and stuffed the rest into his vest pocket.

They rode long that day, stopping to camp next to a creek about a hundred or so yards off the trail. They kept their fire low and cooked some of the thinly cut beef steaks they brought along. Smitty leaned back on his saddle and sighed up at the trees above. "It shore feels good to be back out on the trail." He said to no one in particular. Deke sat back and looked about him. It was a dark night and growing cold. What's the plan, Slate?" asked Heck.

Slate drew a burning twig from the fire and lit his pipe. "I reckon we're gonna patrol the west road a few days ride from here. I got a pretty good idea of the stage lines and schedules, but we'll watch for a few days and maybe once we git the lay of the land

and all we'll help 'em out with offloading some of their valuables."

It was outright robbery and the thought made Heck more than a little nervous. He knew it was the kind of work that would get the law on their heels quicker than anything and could make a fast trip to a low hanging tree branch for a man who got caught. He didn't like it but said nothing.

Deke sat upright and looked intently at the leader. Slate looked at him for a long moment. "There ain't to be no killin' lest it's forced on ya." He insisted.

Smitty guffawed at the comment. "Now you suppose those nice folks will just hand over whatever they got and be glad to do so?"

Slate shook his head "No, I don't Smitty, but the trick is in the bluff. Make 'em think you'll kill them and they'll do as you say. Hell, old man, you ought to know that."

Smitty leaned up on his bony elbows. Let me tell you somethin', Slate; I been a raidin' these roads while you were still draggin on your momma. Don't you go tellin' me what I ought to know!"

The ire rose in Slate's eyes, but he cooled quickly. What Smitty said was true and he knew it. If the job was to get done he needed Smitty's cooperation and he needed everything to run smooth. He decided to pick another trail with the old outlaw.

"That's why we got you along, Smitty. You're an old pro at this and I needed the best to come along on this job."

Smitty blinked, the compliment caught him off guard dousing his indignation with a single splash. "That's good." He said. "You make the plan, Slate, then watch this old man show you how to steal from the rich and give to the poor. The poor bein' us, that is." He smiled at himself.

Deke watched the exchange between the two. The fact that Slate was able to defuse the argument and still maintain the tactical advantage was not lost on him. The following day the gang began a thorough reconnaissance of the miles of road and the surrounding hills, as they rode to the area they were to work.

After four days of searching and watching they selected several spots to hide out. If you were to draw a line connecting them it would zig-zag north and south across the road and continue for miles. The lines would cross the road in likely places to hold up a stage or wagon.

Deception and escape would mean striking in places that were distant from the previous ones. By moving quickly and often, they would have a better chance of outsmarting the posse that would surely be on their tails very soon.

Slate picked the places for ambush and for hideouts with Smitty's help. They took note of telegraph wires and found a few loose poles that a man with a horse and a rope could pull down.

The older man knew the territory well. He had an insight on how people acted and what to expect from a posse. Slate was glad to have him along. He slapped the old outlaw on the back. "You ain't worth a damn as a cattleman." He said with a grin.

Slate and Smitty lay prone on a ridge overlooking the west road. Each held a telescope to their eye. They watched a column of dust rising faintly in the distance. Looking past it, they scanned the back trail and saw no other sign following the approaching stage.

"Ya see that hill right there with the wide spot in the road?" Smitty asked, pointing to a steep rise in the trail. Slate nodded. "They're gonna stop at the top of that rise and let the horses blow. Maybe even have the passengers get out and stretch for a minute. That's the best place to catch 'em."

Slate scanned the area thoroughly. The old man was right. He could see plenty of cover where the gang could conceal themselves until the coach came to a stop.

Smitty pointed out some rocks and brush on both sides of the road. "We'll put a man behind that stand of trees right there and one in them rocks over there." He indicated.

"The man in the rocks will climb to the top and hold a scatter gun on the driver and shotgunner. You come from the trees. Have Heck come from the other side and I'll step out in front and do the talkin'. Deke can take the scattergun position. Once it's all done, have Heck run and yank down that telegraph wire to the east a ways. There's no reason to alert the telegraph folks any sooner than that."

The plan was simple enough and Smitty liked the idea of being the front man. He didn't know about Deke, he thought the boy was too hot headed for that kind of work, but it would be best to have him away from the passengers until they saw how he acted in a hold up. He nodded in agreement. "Thang's can go wrong real quick in this kind of work you make sure to tell that boy to not get too eager on that scattergun."

Slate smirked, knowing the man's concern was well placed. "Alright. Let's get in place." Smitty grabbed Slate's arm. "You oughta tell me what's goin' on here and why the need to come risk our necks on this kind of job."

Slate yanked his arm away and looked at him squarely. "We need to make a big impression on this part of the territory." is all he said. Smitty wasn't satisfied with the explanation, but let it go at that.

The two turned away from their positions and hightailed it down to where the others waited. They briefed them on the plan, Slate issued the warning about shooting. "Keep your fingers off the trigger. No shooting unless you got no other choice."

Smitty checked his pistol as did the others. Smitty handed Deke his shotgun. Deke broke it open, checked the loads, then snapped it back locked. He stuffed a handful of shells into his pocket.

Smitty eyed all of them. "Pull them bandanas over your face and make sure their tight. Don't talk, don't call anybody by name and don't get too close to nobody." The men affixed their disguises.

"Everybody switch hats." Smitty directed. The men paused exchanging curious glances. He looked them over again. "You want to look different than you usually do." He explained as though talking to school children. "Now, switch hats!" The men complied. Trying on each other's hats until they found the one of the others that fit. "I'll do the talkin', ya'll do the work." Smitty said as they moved out to their positions.

The coach swayed down the trail. The horses were in a trot. The driver let them build up some speed before taking on the rise in the road. They made it half-way before the animals began to labor. He flicked the reins clucking at the horses, prodding them on. When they reached the top, he pulled them to a stop to let them catch their breath. He leaned over from his perch and spoke to the passengers inside. "Alright folks, we'll take a few minutes here to let the horses breathe. Step on out and stretch a bit if you've a mind to."

The shotgunner sat upright scanning the area. Something didn't feel right to him. The passengers climbed out of the compartment. There was a man in a dark suit with a pearl tipped lapel pin, a heavy set woman at his side. Two other men stepped out behind them. Both were dressed for travel but were in no other way remarkable.

Smitty stepped from the brush as if taking a Sunday stroll, other than his gun being drawn, and took a hold of the lead horse's bridle. The Shotgunner swung his weapon to bear. "Hold up there, sonny!" Smitty called. Better look around you before you go gettin' yourself killed."

The man looked around. He saw Deke Standing on the rocks, eye-level with his own position. Deke stared down the barrel of the shotgun into the worried eye of the guard. The man eased his shoulders and lowered his weapon. Heck stepped out from the other side, the barrel of his pistol trained on one of the passengers who had hurried to the brush in order to relieve himself. The man's face was beet red, hands held high above, his trousers sagged from an unbuckled belt, his right leg was soaking wet. Heck snickered at the man's predicament as he guided him back to stand with the others.

"These hosse's is mighty tired." Smitty stated to the driver. The driver sneered at the man before him. "Them horses are just fine!" He answered angrily.

Smitty looked the man over. "Looks like ya'll have overloaded this here coach. I reckon we'll have a look at what you got and see if we can't lighten her up a bit for ya! It's just for the sake of these poor over-burdened animals. ya understand."

His gaze turned to the guard. "Now boy you'd better drop that there scatter gun. You make a man kind of nervous." The guard did as directed, tossing the gun to the ground as though it was a useless thing. His jaw was set tight and he glowered at Smitty as he did so.

"There now. We can all get along just fine." Smitty's confidence was contagious, his jovial manner eased the tension in the rest of the gang. "Set that brake good and solid, tie up them ribbons good and tight, then step on down boys. Join the others over there."

Deke held his weapon steady on the two men eyeing the gun belts they both wore. He wondered if Smitty might have overlooked them. The driver and the guard grudgingly followed the orders. When the two men on the seat stepped down Smitty ordered them to drop their gun belts.

"Unbuckle 'em and toss 'em over!" The men angrily complied.

Smitty pointed at Deke directing him by motion to re-position himself to better cover the people at the side of the coach. "How about dropping that box down from behind the seat?" Smitty suggested to the guard.

"I'll do no such thing!" the man retorted.

Smitty stepped in and swatted the man across the temple with the barrel of his gun. The blow knocked the man to the ground, shooting pain through him like a lightning bolt! The heavy woman screamed. "Now looka here, boy!" Smitty called out. "We're right peacable fella's, but if you buck up like that you'll get your horns trimmed quick and hard. You understand that?!"

His voice was harsh as the guard staggered to his feet, pure hatred showing in his face along with the stream of blood that trickled from the wound.

He reached up behind the seat and yanked the box clear letting it topple to the ground. It broke open as it hit. "Ya'll oughta invest in better boxes!" Smitty stated, with a chuckle.

The driver spat between his feet. "We didn't figure on getting robbed." A chuckle rippled through the gang.

The contents were mostly papers. Worthless documents that only held their value in a courthouse or in the conscience of law abiding men. A satchel of gold coins and a stack of paper bills made the action worthwhile, however. Heck scooped them up and stuffed them in a bag. Smitty stood before the people.

"My associates here will now go about your persons. I advise you to stay calm and do not resist.

Whatever you have in your pockets ain't worth dyin' for."

Heck and Slate moved along the line of the passengers. The two men at the end carried nothing but a flask and a few dollars. Slate stepped before the heavy set woman and paused. He wasn't about to put his hands on a woman. She glared at him viciously. She wore a heavy necklace made of pearls and gold beads. He spoke no words but pointed to it and indicated that she remove it and hand it over. Her expression was indignant, but she complied dropping it angrily in his sack.

Smitty looked over at the man in the suit and flipped open the man's jacket. He withdrew a thick wallet from an inside pocket, along with a silver cigar container and matching flask. They were ornately etched and caught the old outlaw's fancy. He plucked the lapel pin from the man's collar.

"Do you have any idea who I am?!" questioned the man, haughtily.

Smitty stepped back and looked him up and down then over at the others. "I figure you're this fat lady's husband!" He answered.

The woman gasped. The man's face turned redder as his anger boiled. Smitty placed his hands on hips. "Do you have any idea who -I- am?" The man held his chin up, his nostrils flared. "I have no earthly idea!"

Smitty smiled big beneath his bandana. "That's good!" He reached out and kicked the man hard in the shin. The man howled and hopped around holding his injured leg. The woman cursed at him "You are a coward, sir! A brute and a coward!"

Smitty eyed her gravely. "Lady don't think I won't kick you just as hard as I did your old man there!" She gasped again but said no more.

Deke stood back with the shotgun the entire time. He enjoyed the display but made sure he kept his eyes on the driver and the guard. When Heck moved to the driver and guard Smitty stopped him. "No not these two, they're hard workin' men. They earned what little they got." Heck shrugged and stepped back.

The guard, still holding his head, glared at the bunch before him. "What the hell would you thievin' low lifes know about hard work?!"

Smitty dropped the barrel of his gun across the driver's forehead. The man grunted and fell to the ground. "What the hell'd you hit me for?!" He screamed. "That's for your partner there! I'd already hit him once and it didn't do much good!" The driver drove a pained and accusatory glance at the guard by his side. The guard gritted his teeth and scowled hard at the outlaw.

"Now let's see what else is in the boot. Why don't you and your pard go ahead and unload that stuff up top." He motioned to the two men on the end. The man with the wet trousers asked in a quivering voice "Can I fasten my britches?" Heck grinned under his mask. The man's plight was comical. "Go ahead." Smitty said.

He hurriedly complied and, along with the other man, climbed up and began tossing down bags and suitcases.

The woman shouted at the men. "Be careful! There are breakables in those bags!"

It wasn't hard to discern the objects of the lady's concern. In a few minutes the powerful scent of an entire bottle of expensive perfume wafted about, emanating from one of her bags that had suddenly grown damp on the bottom.

Heck stepped back trying to escape the powerful fragrance.

"Whew! One of ya'll packin' a skunk along?!" Smitty exclaimed. The lady's face flushed. She shook her head and eyed the outlaw loathing his very existence.

Smitty waved his pistol back and forth across the passengers. "Now ya'll claim your parcels there and put 'em in front of you." The passengers complied. Slate was getting anxious. This was taking too long and Smitty seemed to be enjoying himself too much.

Slate noticed something odd about the form of the other man's waist just above his belt. He eased over to Smitty and whispered something. Smitty nodded in understanding as he eyed the man in question then shook his head. The man's worried eyes met those of the outlaw. Smitty issued a barely noticeable nod and moved his attention elsewhere.

Slate stepped back to his original place. The passenger watched the two. He swallowed hard and became even more nervous. The gang sifted hurriedly through the bags. The man in the suit was reluctant to open his own but did so at the threat of receiving a wound matching the driver and guard.

The inner bags were stuffed with cash and a few small silver bars. A fancy .32 caliber pistol lay on top of the neatly folded clothes. "That's a mighty pretty pistol you got there friend." Smitty said as Heck snatched it up and stuffed it under his belt. "I was hoping to shoot a bandit with it!" replied the man dryly. Smitty looked humorously at him.

"Wa'll, it ain't gonna do you no good locked up in there!"

"Obviously." the man replied flatly. Then he glanced angrily at his wife, "My wife won't let me carry a gun on my person, she says they're too dangerous."

Smitty gave him a sideways look. "More'n likely it'd just give a fella a better reason to kill ya!" Then he nodded at the lady and grinned. "Thank ya Ma'am, it makes our job a lot easier when folks don't get a mind to go shootin' at us!" He laughed.

They finished up their business and Smitty directed the passengers to line up on the side of the road. He ordered the driver to get back in the seat. "Turn that rig around and head back down that hill."

The driver looked confused. "What about them?" He asked.

"They'll keep right here for a bit. Don't go doin' nothing stupid or my friends will start puttin' 'em down." The driver did as he was told. Taking up the reins he coaxed the stage into a tight turn and headed back down the grade.

"I'll see you hang for this!" shouted the man in the suit. Smitty couldn't resist, he stepped abruptly and kicked him in the opposite shin. The man howled even louder than before. His wife broke down and cried.

"Now ya'll just relax." Smitty told them. "We're gonna move on outta here now and leave ya'll to your business."

He motioned for the others to pick up the gun belts and toss them far into the bushes. He noticed the guard's shotgun laying on the ground. He picked it up and admired it. "That's a fine scatter gun you got there, friend. I think I'll take it along so as not to leave too much temptation. Vengeance bein' the Lord's and all..." The guard scowled at him but said nothing.

The gang melted into the woods and hightailed it to their horses. Heck was giggling like a kid as he ran. Once in the saddle they swung toward the hills, spurring their mounts into a run, they split up. Heck sped to the loose telegraph pole, while the others went different directions to join up later at a designated campsite; which had been selected in advance for the cover it provided and its good view of the surrounding area.

From here on out they would have to guard themselves. They all knew it wouldn't be long before the law and a posse of good citizens would be dispatched to trail them.

Deke rode fast on the bay. Filled with excitement, he only wished he could have killed the guard, it would have made the whole thing easier in his estimation. He knew the orders, however, and the heavy hand that would have come down on him had he done it.

Deke rode in right after Smitty. Slate wasn't far behind. He swung down from the saddle and stepped deliberately toward Smitty. He drove an angry finger into the man's chest. "If I thought you was gonna turn that into some kind of sideshow, we would've had a different plan!"

Smitty was taken aback by the confrontation but brushed it off. "You said we needed to make an impression." He replied with a laugh. "Did you see that stuffed shirt when I kicked him in his other leg?" He hooted again.

Slate couldn't deny the humor in the situation. A smile creased his weathered face and he laughed right along with the rest of them. They settled down after a few minutes.

Heck rode in and started in on his tales of the hold up. "You oughta seen that ol' boy's face when I stepped out of them bushes!" He laughed hard, joined by the others.

Slate looked over at Smitty, "Why didn't we take that money belt that other fella wore?" The mention of that caught the others attention quickly and they all turned a questioning eye his way.

Smitty looked a little nervous and even blushed some. "Look here, that young man didn't have much. Did ya'll notice his shoes and his clothes? Did ya see the ring on his finger?" That man had all he ever had and all he could hope for in that belt. He had a wife and maybe a young'un or two that he was tryin' to make a life for."

He paused and looked between the men before him. "I ain't opposed to robbin' a man or even stickin' a knife in his guts if he's got it comin', but I ain't gonna ruin no man that ain't had a chance to make it in the first place."

The old outlaw stood there his hands at sides. He wasn't making any apologies, just stating his position on the matter. The others nodded. They all decided within themselves that it was a standard worth taking hold of. Deke knew too well the struggles of a family trying to make it. He was glad he didn't shoot anybody after all. It was his first outright robbery and he enjoyed it.

Smitty dragged out a blanket and motioning to the others, they dumped their takes in the middle of it. Heck tossed the pistol in. "How about that flask and such ya took from the fat man?" He asked. Smitty withdrew them and looked them over.

"If it's alright with you fella's I'd like to keep 'em for myself. I'll share the contents with ya though."

The men exchanged glances and shrugged. "Why not."

Slate said. "You put on a hell of a show there, but ya did a hell of a job as well. They're yours as a bonus." Smitty smiled. There was enough cigars for everyone, so he passed them around, then he swished the flask around next to his ear. "Dang near full!" He exclaimed.

Deke took a swallow of the contents of the flask when it was passed to him. His cigar made him cough. But he clamped it between his teeth like the others did.

"Smitty?" He asked the old outlaw. "How come you waited to have them fellas drop their guns until they got down?"

Smitty puffed on his cigar and pointed it like a professor giving a lecture. "You don't want a man reaching around his middle when he's sittin' down. He's too close to his guns, and you can't see both sides of him. Make him stand up first. That way he ain't so apt as to roll the dice on grabbin' for 'em."

Deke shrugged. "Makes sense, I guess."

Smitty eyed him sternly. "You're damn right it makes sense."

Tracy T. Thurman

CHAPTER FIVE

Bill Sinclair's method of robbery was far more direct and to the point than his contemporaries, but no less methodical. The big man squatted next to a large pine tree, holding his spyglass to his eye.

The stage depot looked easy. He'd watched it for three days. The schedule was straight forward and didn't vary by more a half hour or so. There were three men there who took care of the place. He placed them by their duties as he surveyed the activities they conducted. There was a front door, of course, that tended to be left open. There were two windows on the side he could see and a back door. A water pump and water trough were to the side of the back door.

He knew the drivers and passengers were fed a meal within the first hour of their arrival. Then they would be on their way again. Soon afterwards, he noticed, the red-haired man would come out the back door, empty a bucket, step to the pump and refill it.

The agent was a tall, thin man with a goatee. He wore a frock coat, a long watch chain and a shoulder holster. The hostler was a stoop shouldered man who appeared to be slow and simple in his mannerisms as well as his thinking. Bill hadn't seen him armed, but thought sure there would a shotgun, pistol or both within easy reach. The other man, average build, red hair, with armbands on his sleeves, was probably a host of sorts, a gambler, bartender, more than likely a petty thief. He was sure to have a hideaway pistol and likely a boot knife.

The stage came in two times a day. One going east, one west. There was a freight rig that stopped by once a day going one direction or the other

The freight rig had well-armed, hard men driving it. He figured on avoiding it unless there was something of real high value on it. Holding up the freight rig would surely mean having to kill the drivers.

It was the last stage he wanted to catch, when the time was right. The passengers and drivers would be tired and sore, not ready to put up much of a fight.

The shotgunner, he noticed, was off his guard at this time. The evening before, he had even left his scatter gun lying on the seat of the rig!

They'd hit the depot first.

Bobby crept up and knelt beside him. "Whatcha thank?" He asked.

Bill withdrew the glass, collapsed it and stowed it in his jacket. "I think we're gonna rob that depot. Then we're gonna rob a stage. Then we're gonna get the hell outta here."

Bobby looked at the big man quizzically. "How you intend to do all that?" He asked.

Bill rubbed his whiskers and looked down at the depot. "I ain't sure just yet. I think you and me ought to go on down there, have a drink, and think it over."

Bobby was stunned. "We oughta what...?"

Bill was visibly growing agitated by the younger man's questions. "We're gonna go inside and have a look around. Just pay attention and don't talk." Bobby nodded in reply. Bill's scowl carried a dire warning.

The two walked into the camp and informed Charlie and Thomas about what they intended. "Ya'll sit tight right here." Bill said. "Don't do anything until we get back."

As they tightened their cinches to go, Bill asked Bobby, "Can you walk with a limp?"

"A limp?"

"Yeah, a limp. Can you walk with a limp?"

Bobby shook his head and hobbled around as if his leg didn't work right.

"No. that won't do." Bill replied. He stepped over and swung his fist down hard and low, striking Bobby on the outside of his thigh! The younger man all but went down.

"OW! Son of a...! What the hell'd you go and do that for!" He hollered, hobbling around for real.

Bill grinned in reply. "Bet you can limp now."

Bobby rubbed his leg. A large knot swelled up in it, a knot just about the size of Bill's fist. "Son of a..., damn that hurt!"

Bill nodded, "I'm sure it did, all part of the plan. Keep your hat pulled down low and your mouth shut!"

The two men sauntered their horse to the hitch rail in front. There were two windows, one each side of the door. They dismounted and walked up the steps.

Bobby limping behind as they went. The door was open, and they stepped inside.

The interior was clean and orderly, save for a light coating of dust. The red-haired man leaned against the bar, idly flipping cards over. The man Bill had pegged as the agent sat at a large, fancy desk in a separate room eyeing some ledgers, a long cigar smoldering in an ashtray next to him.

The door was propped open with a rock. A single window with a shade over it was to the agent's right. The hostler, he knew, was outside in the bar, probably where he spent the majority of his time.

"Howdy." the red-haired man spoke. Bill nodded in greeting. "Name's Steven. What can I get for you?" He continued.

Bill eased up to the bar on the right side of the room. In length, it was a short bar, but it served its purpose in the limited space and for the few customers of the place. The red-haired man stepped behind the bar and placed his hands in front of him, a fake smile on his face.

"How about a couple whiskeys?" Bill responded. Bobby was surprised by the jovial tone of Bill's speech.

"Sure thing" the red-haired man said. He brought out two glasses, set them on the bar and filled them with amber liquid.

Bill fumbled in his pocket, loosening a gold watch as he did so. He placed a few dollars on the bar and picked up his glass, Bobby picked his up only afterward.

The younger man noticed Bill's watch dangling loosely from his vest pocket. He wanted to mention it but thought better of it.

"Where ya'll coming from or going to?" the red-haired man asked.

Bill eased around side to side a bit as if he were stretching his back. Making sure the stranger got a good view of his loose pocket watch. "Oh, nowhere special really. Maybe find some work up north before the money runs out." He answered.

Bobby caught the idea that Bill was playing this fellow and figured he'd better keep his lip buttoned and his eyes open.

Steven stepped around the bar with the bottle in hand and took a chair at a table. "Why don't you fellas join me and get comfortable?"

Bill nodded and motioned to Bobby to play along.

The man pulled a chair out as Bill sat down. He offered his hand. "I'm Steven." He stated.

Bill shook the man's hand. "Joe, an' this here's Nelson." Bobby nodded warily.

"Your friend don't talk much does he?"

"Nope, he's a little slow ya know. Got run over by a wagon when he was a kid. Ain't usually got much to say." Bobby couldn't help but stick his lip out a little.

The two began talking about nothing in particular. Bill looked around with an appreciative expression. "This is a nice place ya'll got here."

The red haired man nodded and refilled Bill's glass. If Bill was trying to pose himself as an easy target he was doing a fine job. The red haired man welcomed the game. "Yup." He said. "We like to keep it neat and tidy for the stage line customers and passersby like yourselves." The man's colloquial speech wasn't fooling anyone.

The agent stepped from his office, walked past the table with no recognition that anyone was there. He stepped to the door and to the left side of the porch. "Lem!" He called. "Lem! Come in!"

Bill and Bobby sat upright exchanging cautious glances.

The man stepped back in. He was a tall slender man. There was an aloof air about him. Still, he paid no mind to the men in the room. Lem, the hostler, stepped in and swept the hat from his head. The tall man smiled at him. "Lem, I need to know how much feed is left in the barn. Can you tell me that?"

Lem nodded. "There're twenty-four one-hundred pound sacks." He stated matter of factly.

The tall man nodded in return. "Thank you, Lem. I know I can always count on you. I'll holler at you again around supper time."

Lem nodded again and turned out the door, flopping his hat back in place and stepping his way back to the barn.

"Who's that?" Bill inquired.

"Oh that's Mr. Roger Appleton." He replied with a flourish of his hand. "He's the agent here. He don't care about nothing but the numbers on the clock and in his ledgers. The other fella is actually his nephew. Works as a hostler here. A nice enough fella, but kinda touched if ya know what I mean." The last words, he spoke in a low voice, his eyes shifting momentarily to Bobby.

Bobby sipped his drink sparingly and looked around the place as best he could without being too obvious.

There was a pot-bellied stove on the back wall just to the right of the office door. The room was cut back into another open space where there was a kitchen of sorts and where the back door was. A gun rack with three Winchesters hung off to the left side it. He noticed another rifle leaning by the door and was sure there would be a shotgun under the bar. Bill was on his third drink and was showing signs of intoxication. Odd. Bobby thought. Bill could gulp that whole bottle without burping if he wanted to. When he'd tossed back the last of his drink, he sat the glass down purposefully on the table.

"Well, he said as he rose from his chair. We'd better get going." Bobby finished off his own drink and stood up.

The red haired man looked disappointed. "You oughta stay and play some cards." He exclaimed. "We'll have a coach coming in later, there'll be grub and folks who'll want a good poker game."

Bill smiled and shook his head." Sorry, my friend, gotta keep moving. Thanks for the invite, maybe we'll stay longer next time. Yes, sir." He said looking around and smiling. "Next time… for sure."

He gave Bobby a narrow stare and the two walked out. Bobby's limp was still working just fine. As they rode away, Bobby noticed Bill's watch was missing.

"Hey Bill, I think you lost your watch." Bill smirked. "I know, but I'll get it back." He said menacingly. "I'll get it back and then some…"

Bobby's leg still hurt. They lay low that night. Bobby rubbed some horse liniment on his bruised thigh. Charlie and Thomas played cards on a horse blanket.

Bill was stretched back, head on his saddle, twirling a piece of straw in his teeth. His mind was formulating a plan, searching out the possibilities and trying to figure every angle. One thing he was sure of. Steven was going to get skinned down to his long johns!

He laid out the plan the next morning. He went over the normal schedule of the depot as well as the inner lay out of the place.

"These fellas ain't gonna be too hard to handle. If we do it right" Bill explained. "The slick one might try something to save his own hide but ya'll leave that sumbitch to me. As for the agent, those sorts can be dangerous. He's a company man and has more pride than sense." Bill continued.

"Disarm him as quick as you can and get him tied to a chair or something. The hostler's another one to watch. There's no telling what he might do, but he might also be an ace in the hole. I don't want no killin', ya'll understand?

There will be a cash box in the office we'll get, and probably one behind the bar. Leave the agent and the hostler alone, except for any weapons they got. The slick one with the red hair's mine to handle."

The freight wagon clattered away an hour after it arrived. The drivers had been fed, and fresh mules had been harnessed. The gang sat tight for another hour afterwards. Then Bill prepared to disperse the men.

"Bobby, you and me will ease up to the back door. When that slick red-headed fella comes out, stick your pistol in his ear and steer him around real quiet. Charlie, you and Thomas go on in and take the far table to the left and wait. Make some noise, just enough to bother the agent.

The boys nodded. Sweat was already running down Bobby's back.

It didn't take long for them to get into place. Bobby eyed the barn hoping Lem wouldn't see them. Bill had an amused expression on his face. He was looking forward to this.

The back door swung open almost as if on cue. Steven stepped out unaware. A thin cigar hung from his lip. "Hold it!" Bobby commanded as he placed the barrel of his pistol against Steven's ear. Steven froze in place, raising his arms cautiously. "Turn around and go back in real slow and quiet like."

Bill stepped in front of Steven just then. A wicked smile etched across his face. "Good to see you again." He hissed.

As they stepped in, they could hear a ruckus going on in the main room. Charlie and Thomas were moving chairs around and hollering for service. Bill whispered to Steven, call that agent man out here. Nice and easy like you just want to ask him a question or somethin'."

Steven cleared his throat his mouth had gone awful dry. "Uh, Mr. Appleton?" He called out meekly. They could hear the man curse as he rose in aggravation from his desk.

"What is it this time?" He exclaimed before he left his office. "Steven, can't you even do one thing..." He rounded the corner of the room and walked right into Bill's gun.

Bill cocked the hammer back. "I'll drop you where you stand!" He threatened.

Roger Appleton's hand went up in the same fashion as his associate. Bill flung his coat open and removed the pistol from the shoulder holster. It was an ornate weapon, a gentleman's gun, to be sure. Bill tucked it away in his own belt. "Stand with your face against that wall there, and keep those hands reaching up!" Bobby held his gun on them as well.

The agent protested. "You'll have no luck here!" He exclaimed. "The company will track you down and hang you from the nearest tree!"

Charlie grabbed the man and forced him into a chair. With Thomas' help they tied him good and snug. "Keep quiet and we won't stuff a rag in your mouth." Charlie warned.

Bobby knew Steven still had a gun and probably a knife somewhere on his person. He wondered if Bill had forgotten. He didn't. Bill grabbed Steven by his neck and flung him against a table, toppling the chairs in the process. "Give me back my watch, you weaselly bastard!"

Steven staggered to his feet, his hand was quick reaching for the pistol in his waistband. It was just the move Bill wanted him to make. He stepped into him swinging his fist high and hard, the impact against Steven's cheek bone split the skin wide open.

The derringer flew from his hand and skittered harmlessly out of reach. Bill swung again, and a third time. Steven crumpled to the floor in a heap. He motioned to Thomas. "Yank his boots off."

Thomas did as he was told. The left boot had a long skinny knife in a narrow sheath sewn to the inside. Bill grabbed the man by the nape of his neck and sat him down forcefully in a chair. "Tie him up." He commanded. Ropes went around Steven's wrists and chest securing him in place. Bobby stepped behind the bar. He withdrew a shotgun, placing it on the bar, and a cigar box containing a small sum of money, as well as a handkerchief containing odds and ends of various value. He held up Bill's watch smiling. "Found it!"

He turned to the agent. "Call in your hostler." The man ignored him. Bill's open hand swatted him across the face. "Call in your hostler!"

The agent looked away, his chin wavered. "He's no threat to you, just leave him be."

Bill leaned to eye level with the man. "He ain't gonna be hurt if he comes in peaceable. He will get hurt if he don't though."

The man swallowed hard. "I'll need to go to the door."

Bill motioned to Thomas and Charlie. The two men carried the tied down agent to the door, chair and all.

"Now you call him just like you did yesterday. Say anything wrong and I'll kill him, then you."

The agent nodded nervously. "L-Lem! Come in, Lem!"

Bill watched the man emerge from the barn and tread to the house.

"Carry him back over there." He ordered. Bobby stood behind the door.

When Lem entered and pulled his hat off. Bobby raised his gun. The man froze; his eyes wide glancing around in confusion.

"Uncle?" He questioned.

The agent spoke softly. "It's okay, Lem, they won't hurt you. Come on in and sit down." Lem complied, although his legs were shaky. Charlie tied him in place just as the others.

"Good job." Bill said. "You're safe as long as you cooperate. Where's the cash box?" The agent ignored him. "Bobby, go in there and check that office. Bobby complied, sorting through papers and books. He slid open drawers, spilling the contents, as he went. The agent grimaced at the racket Bobby was making.

"This bottom drawer is locked."

"Well bust it open! Use that rock, there, by the door!" Bill ordered.

The agent spoke up. "Please, that's an antique desk, it was my father's desk. I implore you, don't destroy it."

Bobby stopped his actions.

"Where's the key then?" Bill demanded.

The agent looked defeated. "It-It's in my left coat pocket."

Charlie reached in and found the key. There was also a silver watch with a chain and a medallion. Charlie took the key, tossed it to Bobby and held up the watch, admiring it greedily.

Bill snatched it from his hand. He flipped the cover. A picture of a very lovely woman adorned the inside. "Who's the lady?" Bill asked, appreciating her graceful features.

"My wife. That's my wife." the agent replied.

Bill tucked the watch back into the agent's pocket. "You're a lucky man." He said. The agent wore a solemn expression.

Bobby opened the bottom drawer of the desk and found a metal box. He pried open the lid. There was a thick stack of bills and a handful of gold and silver coins. He showed Bill, who nodded in satisfaction. As he went out, he kicked the rock that held the door, it swung out into the doorway, revealing a safe in the corner. "Well, well. Bobby stated. There's a safe in here."

Bill's attention returned to the agent. "You're gonna open that safe." The man attempted to ignore him again." Bill rolled his eyes. "You're going to open that safe!" Bill demanded as he struck the agent in the same manner as before.

Lem yelped and struggled at his ropes. Thomas placed his hand firmly on his shoulder. Still, the agent said nothing. Bill drew the hammer on his pistol and placed against Steven's head. "You'll open that safe or I'll splatter this bastard's brains out!"

The agent took notice then, sneered in reply. "You'd be doing the world a favor."

Bill was tempted to pull the trigger anyway, just for his own satisfaction. He stepped to Lem and repeated the process.

The man clenched his eyes tight, hunkered his shoulders and wheezed in fear.

The agent glared up at the big outlaw with venom in his eyes. "You wouldn't dare!"

Bobby spoke up quickly stepping into the agent's view. "Yes. Yes, he would. And he wouldn't bat an eye doing it!"

The agent swallowed hard shifting his eyes to Bobby, to Lem, then back at Bill.

"Okay! Okay, I'll open the safe. But you must take what you have and leave here!"

Bill leaned over to eye level again. "It doesn't look like you're as interested in your luck holding out as you should be." He withdrew the watch from the agent's pocket. Opening it, he held it front of him.

"Are you sure you're in the position to try to give me orders?" He hissed.

The agent looked sadly at the picture then to Bill's angry face. "She died in childbirth five years ago..."

Bill made no reply. Closed the watch and replaced it in the man's pocket. He re-evaluated the agent, however.

"I'll open the safe." the agent repeated.

Thomas untied him. He rose, rubbing his wrists. Bobby's gun was in his back as they walked to the safe. "You make a single wrong move mister, and you'll die right where you are." He warned.

The agent knelt in front of the big iron box and spun the combination. Presently, he unlatched the door and pulled it ajar.

Bobby pulled him aside. Inside was a large stack of bills, bags of coins and a stack of gold bars. Bobby's eyes grew wide at the contents. "Hot damn!" He exclaimed. There were also stacks of legal papers and a Remington revolver. "It's a good thing you didn't try to reach for that gun." He warned the agent. The tall man sat splayed out in a chair. A bruise shone on his cheek and his left eye was swelling. He only nodded. He was exhausted, broken, and defeated.

"The stage'll be here soon." Bobby said. The gang shoved the proceeds of the robbery into sacks. The gold bars were small, heavy and awkward. They sure weren't going to leave them, however.

"Alright." Bill said. "We'll let the stage alone for now. Let's go." He paused when he looked at the battered Steven. He was conscious, but not by much.

He pointed to Thomas. "Go out there to the barn and bring up a horse." He yanked the man up from his chair then dropped him on the floor. With Charlie's help he stripped him of everything short of his underwear.

The two men dragged him to the back and shoved him over the horse's back, tying him in place. Bill pointed the animal out toward the flatlands and gave it a vicious slap on the rump! The animal jumped and bolted, running for its life into the sagebrush and brambles, its passenger bouncing on its back. The men collectively laughed at the scene. They went inside to finish things up.

"You are a brute, sir." the agent stated. Bill made no reply. The agent looked around him. The place had been turned upside down. Everything of value taken. Failure consumed him. He was morose and bewildered. "What will I tell the company...?"

Bill grabbed a bottle and a glass from behind the bar and placed it before him. "That's your problem." He said. He filled a glass and handed to the agent. "Have a drink."

Lem looked around, his lip trembled, but he gave no indication of stirring. Charlie and Thomas brought their horses up. They mounted quickly, spurring their mounts to the hills.

Roger Appleton Esquire sat in his ruined stage depot. He had freed his nephew Lem from his bonds and offered him a drink. He drank his fifth glass of whiskey, then stood, walked over to where Steven's derringer lay on the floor and picked it up. He withdrew his watch and gazed at the photo held within. He then turned to his nephew. "I am sorry, Lem." He stated, then stepped out on the front porch, placed the weapon against his temple and pulled the trigger.

The gang stopped at the top of the hill. A column of dust emanated from the horizon. "That would be the stage." Bobby said. Bill withdrew his spyglass and scanned the station. He sat bolt upright and cursed. "What is it?" Bobby queried.

Bill handed his glass over his jaw clenched tight. Bobby scanned the depot back to front, then stopped. He could see the form of a fallen man on the front porch. A man wearing a long frock coat. "I'll be damned." Bobby exclaimed. "The damn fool walked out there and shot himself in the head." Bill growled. "They'll lay that on us shore as hell. The damn fool."

They kicked their mounts into a run. They needed a lot of space between them and where they presently were.

Tracy T. Thurman

CHAPTER SIX

While the two gangs were plying their trade in the wilderness, Carl, Cotton and two hands from the home ranch, Pedro, and Raymond, sequestered themselves in a town just north of the border.

The latter two were not aware of the silver and were more or less average hands on the ranch. They were by no means what one would call 'honest men', but they weren't professional outlaws either. To their knowledge, they were simply there to buy cattle.

Mescolare was a dusty little town of no particular importance, other than a road and a ferry that carried people, wagons, stock, and supplies across the river.

Carl watched the goings on with interest. He made it a point to read the newspapers as they became available. The hotel they stayed in was prompt in making sure their guests had the latest available copies. He sat on a bench on the hotel veranda, his feet propped on an old stump someone had placed there for that purpose. He scanned the paper in his hands. The headline caught his attention.

"BANDITS!" The word was printed in large, bold type. He read the account of a stage held up on a road north and west of the town. It told of a group of men, four or five, of indeterminable origin with their faces covered, who robbed the east bound stage. "The men brutally assaulted the driver, the guard and one of the passengers; a prominent businessman and financier. The bandits made off with a wealth of stolen goods."

The story described how the passengers were subjected to insults and "grievous improprieties". Carl passed the paper over to Cotton as he took a place next to him on the bench. "It seems old Slate's doing a good job on his end.

Cotton scanned the article. His lips moved as he read. "That'll get the birds a flyin." He stated. They sat and surveyed the traffic in the street.

Watching the ferry, Carl determined it had no certain schedule. It worked as the business provided itself. Now and then, however, it would wait for a full load to make its trek across the water. He watched with a furrowed brow when he saw a group of men cross. These were not average pilgrims. They were hard men with the look of killers on them.

Carl elbowed Cotton who was snoozing next to him, hat pulled over his eyes. He sat up and nudged his hat brim up. The riders were five in number. They looked like vaqueros and would likely pass as such to the average citizen. They wore red sashes around their waists, wide sombreros and rancho clothes, adorned in the fashion of their culture. Carl and Cotton both could clearly see these were men looking for something in particular.

"I think a fly just landed in the soup." Cotton stated.

Carl nodded. "I'd count five flies to be exact."

They watched as they rode by. He eyed the brands on the horses. It was familiar, but there was something different about it. Many brands had similarities, but this one was too close to the original Molina rancho brand, a fancy "M" with curved appendages and a cross emanating upwards from the crux of the letter. This one had the same "M" but a rising sun above it. He studied it curiously.

It didn't take long for the men to take notice of them. The leader, his dark face expressionless studied them as he went by, placed his hand on the butt of his pistol and nodded.

The movement would have been barely perceptible to anyone else. It spoke volumes however, to the men sitting on the veranda. Carl took note, and simply nodded back, the shadow of his hat brim barely moving.

"Where's Pedro?" Carl asked.

"Over at the livery I think. Him and Raymond seem to like it there."

Carl replied. "Get him. I'll be upstairs. Come in the back way."

Cotton rose from his seat and stepped off into the veranda.

The vaqueros ambled down the street and tied their horse in front of the cantina. They glared back at the gringos momentarily before entering the establishment.

There was a tap on the door. "Yeah." Carl answered.

The door eased open. Pedro stepped in along with Cotton. "You wanted to see me boss?"

Carl stood by the window and pulled the curtain back. "You see those horses in front of the cantina?"

Pedro looked and nodded. "Si"

"Do you recognize any of them or the brand?"

Pedro peered again, squinting his eyes. "I don't know the horses. But I think I know the brand. Muy bad."

Cotton and Carl exchanged sober glances. "Pedro, go down there and nose a round a little. See what you can find out." Carl instructed.

"Si," Pedro replied as he turned out of the room.

Carl watched from the window as Pedro walked across the dusty street and made his way to the cantina. Cotton sat in a chair and rolled a cigarette. "Damn it!" He exclaimed. Carl agreed with him.

Pedro walked into the cantina, pausing inside the door to dust his boots off. He walked to the bar and ordered a beer. The bartender was a big Mexican man with a long beard. He had a patch over one eye, his soiled shirt stretched over his belly.

He pushed the dusty mug over with no words. Pedro nodded and laid some coins on the bar. The bartender's big paw swept them into his other and dropped them in a can. He walked to the other end where the vaqueros Carl had mentioned stood. He saw the bartender say something to one of them, then saw the man's gaze lock onto his own. The vaquero was tall and slim. He had a long mustache and eyes that were dark as night. His clothes were of a better cut and quality than those of the others.

Pedro thought he looked familiar but couldn't place him. The tall vaquero took two glasses and a bottle in hand and walked down to stand beside Pedro. He leaned close to him, almost touching. He sat the glasses and filled them, sliding one to Pedro.

He took his glass in hand and held it. Pedro did the same. "Salute."

"Salute." Pedro replied. He was growing nervous, then the tall man spoke. Quietly, almost politely, but with an air of threat in his voice.

"Tell me, my friend. Why do you ride with those gringos?"

Pedro swallowed hard. The tall man filled his glass again. Pedro hesitated to pick it up for fear his hand would tremble. "They are my employers." He said, knowing he couldn't lie and get away with it.

The man looked him up and down. "What are they doing here?" He asked with the same tone.

"Buying cattle, looking for some grazing land." Pedro exclaimed.

The man laughed. "Men like that don't buy cows."

Pedro shrugged. "That is all I know."

The man filled Pedro's glass again. "He sent you here to spy on us. Did he not?"

Pedro tried to act innocent. "No one sent me here! I go where I please."

The man smirked. "Do you know who I am?"

Pedro had an idea, but he wasn't going to admit it. "No Señor." He answered flatly.

The man's countenance changed to one of raw malevolence. "You will find out soon, peon. Hope you don't find out the hard way." He sneered at Pedro as if he were something unclean. Yet, he filled his glass again. "Finish your drink, peon, then go!"

Pedro gulped down the tequila and turned to go. His ears burned as he hurried down the walk. He didn't go straight to Carl, but instead to the livery where he knew he could find Raymond. He was there, playing a game of chess with the stockman.

"What's going on pard?" Raymond asked.

"I-I don't know. I think we'd better go Raymon'."

Raymond was taken back. "Leave. What are you talking about?"

Pedro looked at the stockman who was probably someone who didn't need to know anything else. "I-I don't know." Pedro was downright frightened and that was a rare thing.

Raymond stood up, "Let's go back to the hotel, have a drink and talk to the boss."

Pedro paced back and forth. "Okay, okay, let's go, Raymon'." The two left the livery in a hurry.

Raymond had to almost run to keep up with his friend.

Inside Carl's room, Pedro sprawled in a chair his face fraught with worry. Cotton poured him a glass full of whiskey and placed it in his hand. The fact that a man like Pedro could be shaken in that manner was a confirmation of what they suspected.

"He knew who I was." Pedro said, gulping his drink. "I know these men, these Molinas..." Carl knew them too. By reputation mostly. The Molina Rancho was an old Spanish grant. It was a dynasty of generations and one that operated with an iron fist. Not even the Army would cross their land without permission.

Pedro swallowed the last of the liquor and sat his glass down firmly on the table. "I think we should leave boss. There are no cows here!" He spat those last words as if the taste of them was sour. In his angst, Pedro was growing angry.

"Calm down Pedro..." Carl said. "We ain't goin no place. Go on back to the livery, keep your ears and eyes open and your mouth shut. Molina might have us at a disadvantage for now. But let's see how this shakes out."

Pedro looked over at Raymond, then back to his boss. "Okay, if you say so."

The two ranch hands left. Their minds swirling with worry and questions. "Don't worry, pard'." Raymond said to his friend. "Old Carl ain't never let us down before."

Pedro continued his fast walk. "Si, I know Raymon', but this is different. Keep your pistola loose."

Cotton handed Carl a newspaper. It was a few days old, but the information it held was of grave concern.

"Murder and brutality!" the headline read. The story told of a stage depot that was robbed. "Four brazen men attacked the Appleton Stage Depot." it began. It told of a vicious assault resulting in the death of two men. That of the agent, a notable Mr. Roger Appleton Esquire, "A fine, upstanding man of impeccable moral principles and the widowed son in law of territorial senator Malcom Edwards."

It went on and described an emptied safe and ransacked interior. "The remains of another citizen were found tied to a horse which had fallen with a broken leg. The victim apparently beaten and driven mercilessly into the brambles and sage of the wilderness!

Immediate identification was not readily available, but itis believed to be that of a Steven

Florence, a gentleman of integrity and a host employed by the stage line."

Carl slapped the folded paper against his leg. "Damn it, Bill!" He spat. He met Cotton's gaze. "Let's go get supper."

The two men sat a table, their dinners complete. They drank their coffee from porcelain cups that were too small. The door opened, and the tall vaquero walked in, another man faintly resembling the first entered behind him.

They walked to the table where Carl and Cotton sat. Drawing out chairs, they sat without a word.

"Have a seat." Carl said.

A tense moment passed, the men exchanged wary glances that held both recognition and challenge. The second man locked eyes on Cotton who did the same in reply. He tapped his finger on the butt of his gun. Cotton smirked with an amused expression.

The leader smiled, placed his arms folded on the table and leaned toward Carl. The later held his position coolly but made a quick mental calculation as to how fast he could get to his gun. "I know why you are here gringo." He said, almost whispering.

Carl leaned back, adjusting his seat enough to clear his sidearm just a bit more. "That a fact?" He replied. "Why don't you tell me why you think I am here?"

The man's smile never changed. "It sure as hell is not to buy cattle, Señor."

Carl matched the man's smile but said nothing, allowing him to pick the trail.

The man's English was perfect, flavored with a rich Spanish accent. The man leaned back then. "I know who you are, Señor Ferguson."

"And I know who you are, Señor Molina."

Molina leaned back and spread his arms. "Then why do we play these games?"

Carl decided to get to the point but wanted to walk around it a bit first. "I see you changed your brand."

Molina smiled again. "Yes! You like it!" He said in feigned concern of Carl's opinion. "There is a story behind it which I will tell you if we don't start shooting each other first."

Molina was not pleased that his presence didn't have the effect on these men as he thought it should. He knew however, that if it had, he would have been disappointed and much less inclined to further the discussion. "You want the silver that is coming from Mexico. Is that right, Señor Ferguson?"

Carl made no indication in the affirmative or negative but held his cool countenance.

Molina sat back and tilted his head. "Señor, we are intelligent men. Why don't we speak plainly?"

Carl nodded and shrugged. "Alright. Speak as plain as you are willing to do. I'll listen until you're finished."

The burden of the conversation rested on Molina now and he didn't like it, but he persisted. He leaned forward again as he did so, he took notice of the icy glare between his compadre and Cotton. "Now don't be rude, brother..." He said. "These are reasonable men. Let's be reasonable also." The man shifted his eyes away.

Cotton did the same. The two, however, kept the other well within their peripheral vision.

"Let's start again, Señor Ferguson; I am Miguel Molina of the Molina Rancho, this is my brother, Juan." He said, with an elaborate graciousness."

Carl sat up straight his smile unchanged, deciding to play along with Molina's scheme just to see where it led. "My name is Carl Ferguson." He said, "This is my associate, Cotton Joe."

Molina smiled again. "There. Now let's get down to the business of why you are here, and why I am here."

Carl leaned forward on the table, his hat brim inches away from the brim of Miguel's sombrero. "You're doin' the talkin'." He said.

"Yes, of course. The silver you are after belongs to my family. It is very old and it belongs to the Molina Rancho."

Carl considered his words for a moment. "And you want to make sure it gets there. Right?"

Miguel sat up and raised his hand. "That is where you are wrong. I will make sure it doesn't. At least not yet."

Carl and Cotton exchanged questioning glances. "I don't understand."

"You see, my uncle, Raul Molina, has taken the rancho. My father died, and I am the rightful heir. But my uncle is a snake! He moved in before my father was even in his tomb! My uncle banished me. He disinherited me. He even tried to have me excommunicated!" He emphasized his last statement by crossing himself in the manner of men in his belief do.

"Why did he want to do all that?!" Cotton asked.

Miguel shrugged. "Because I killed his son. His son was an evil man. Even worse than his father. Whom I will kill too. Eventually. That is why I changed my brand you see. I added the rising sun because I am the rising son of the Molina Rancho! I want it seen and known." He punctuated his statement by driving his finger tip into the table. He then sat back folding his arms in front of himself, allowing a moment to let his words sink in.

Carl raised his eyebrows. Visually impressed with Miguel's story. "I see, but what's that got to do with us?"

"Everything Señor. You see, I can't allow you to steal my silver, my treasure!"

"What makes you think you can stop me...?"

Miguel sat back eyeing Carl coldly. "I will explain this to you one time, Señor, although I am very sure you have already considered it. You have four men here. I have five. Your other two men are not fighters. That leaves only you two. All of my men are fighters, Señor, all of them. I have many, many more. I have an army. I need that silver."

Carl could see the writing pretty clearly. He wasn't one to pull in his horns however.

Miguel continued. "You see, Señor Ferguson, we can fight you and win very easily. But that serves us no purpose. We will kill you, you will kill some of us. You might even kill me. But I will surely kill you. I know you have other men who will come here. We will kill them also. Where will that leave us? Huh? Where? We will make a lot of noise and bring the law and the American Federalies to complicate things even more. My uncle would win without a fight. My rancho, my father's and grandfather's legacy would sink into ruin!" Miguel held his hands out. "I simply don't have time to fight another battle. I would rather have you as an ally. I need good, strong allies much more than I need another enemy. And you my friend, will also have a strong ally."

Carl contemplated Miguel's story. He truly felt an urge to shift his position and partner up with him. He knew nothing of fighting for a family's honor. His own never had any to speak of. The thought intrigued him. He was cautious however.

Getting into another man's war is asking a lot. He had a lot on the line and he wasn't about to take any unnecessary chances. Trust is a mighty hard thing to come by in their particular line of work.

"And we help you, then you turn your guns on us. I know how that sort of agreement usually works out." Carl said the words flatly, tapping his finger on the table. Cotton Joe nodded in agreement.

Miguel shook his head. "Ah, Señor Ferguson, it is clear you don't know me as well as you think. Of many things, I am first a man of honor. My word is iron. I expect the same from others as well." Carl caught a hint of warning in that last sentence but ignored it. Miguel nudged his brother. "Tell him, Juan. Tell him of our honor." He said proudly.

Juan's face looked as if it was lined with years of anger. He nodded heavily. "The honor of the Molina's is never in question. That is why my brother, and I must take back our rancho. Our uncle has dishonored it, and us. And that, is the worst of offenses. We do not betray our given word."

Carl considered all that was said. He believed Miguel was telling the truth, though he questioned if the man's faculties were completely intact. He had heard of trouble at the Molina Rancho, but it was so far away, he paid it no mind. It interested him now. What he did from this moment on would likely change everything. He sure as hell wasn't about to turn tail and run though. "Tell me what you have in mind, Miguel."

Miguel smiled nudging his brother who did the same. "Later! Let's have drinks. We will meet tomorrow. It will give us both time to think." He ordered a bottle of Champagne. An odd choice Carl thought. He didn't personally like the stuff, but the Molina's were more of a refined people.

Juan withdrew a newspaper from inside his jacket and laid it on the table. "We were surprised to find you here." He said. "We thought you were working in the north."

Carl's eye fastened on the headline. "Another Stage Robbed! Troops Dispatched to Quell the Violence!" He sat his glass down, glad to be away from the foul tasting Champagne and picked up the paper. "I'd like to take this." He said.

Juan waved his hand. "It is yours."

Miguel chimed in, touching his temple. "Diversions. Very smart, Señor, very smart. This will work well."

Juan picked up Carl's glass, refilled it, and handed it back to him, smiling as he did so. He had a broken front tooth. Carl tried not to frown. Cotton Joe licked his lips and held his glass for another refill.

Tracy T. Thurman

CHAPTER SEVEN

Slate and Smitty watched the sharp bend in the road. The stage slowed as it approached. It was a blind corner that was cut into a hill on the inside of the turn and passed an opposing bend in a creek on the outside.

"That's a good place right there." Smitty exclaimed. "Ya see how they slow almost to a walk? The driver and guard don't know what's there until they're already on it."

Slate watched the coach meander around the bend. He watched the mannerisms of the driver and guard. They appeared to be alert. But, not exceedingly so. It was indeed a good place for a holdup. He studied it with a tactical eye. "We'll post a man atop that hill right there. Not right off, but soon as we get the rig halted. We'll do pretty much as before. We'll have Heck on the inside of the turn to watch the guard, then have him go up on the hill to watch out. You do what you do up front. Me and Deke'll work the passengers."

Smitty rolled the thought around in his jaw like a cud for minute. He still wasn't too sure about the younger man being up close to the passengers. He mentioned so to Slate.

"Yeah, he'll be fine. I'll be right there. I'd rather have Heck on the hill."

Smitty nodded. "Okay, if that's how you want to play it. It's fine by me. I want to watch that coach a few miles or so before we go at it. Get a better idea of who we might be dealin' with."

Slate agreed. "You'll have to be movin' fast."

"Won't be a problem." Smitty replied.

The two men motioned for the others to join them and shared the plan pointing out each man's positions and duties. "We'll catch the stage about this time tomorrow." Smitty grinned. "Sure beats pushin' cows around don't it?" Deke's grin almost matched that of the elder man.

Smitty picked a smooth trail, as direct as he could, between the intended hold up place and a washout in the road. They'd have to slow down to navigate the rough, rutted area, enough so the outlaw could get a good look at the passengers and estimate the strength of any guns on board.

He sprawled on an opposing rise and spied on the coach from a distance. It slowed down just as he thought. The driver and guard were just as they should be. Stage men hired to do a job. The passengers consisted of two men and perhaps three women. He couldn't make them out as much as he wished but he could clearly see there weren't any soldiers or lawmen on board. He scrambled from his hiding place, leapt into the saddle and high tailed it to where the others were waiting.

"Alright, they'll be here shortly. Ya'll know what you're supposed to do!" They had already pulled on their bandanas and swapped hats. Heck Braden took his place mid-way up the hill inside the turn. Smitty, Deke, and Slate spaced themselves on the outside of the road and waited. The sound of the approaching coach told of its proximity.

The driver leaned back on the reins, the horses wavered slowing their trot to a walk. The driver and guard had made the same trip numerous times. They knew the bend only as a landmark telling them they were about halfway to the next station.

Smitty stepped out, gun drawn and took hold of the lead horse's halter. "Hold up there!" He hollered.

The driver was a big man who wore a gray beard striped with tobacco stains. He had large arms that protruded from rolled-up sleeves. He flipped the reins on the horses' back urging them to run. The horses bucked in response almost causing Smitty to lose his grip. He pointed his pistol at the driver ordering him to, "Hold them horses!"

Heck, who stood not ten feet from the guard and just a little higher, saw what was happening. He aimed the shotgun directly at the guard's face. "Stop that wagon or I'll splatter you all over your partner there!"

The guard froze and reached his arm across the driver prompting him to halt the team. The horses settled down presently. Smitty released the halter. He was mad clear through. "Get those folks outta there!" He commanded. "And climb your asses down off that box!"

Slate watched Smitty with caution knowing a cool head was needed and Smitty didn't have that right now.

Deke stepped out and yanked open the stage door. His gun held steady on the passengers. Slate covered the door from the left.

Heck held his weapon on the driver and guard. They had their hands up, but it was clear they hadn't made up their minds about the options of making a fight.

"Drop that scatter gun!" Smitty ordered the guard. The man set his jaw and hesitated.

Heck moved another foot or two closer making sure he saw the barrels of his shotgun pointed straight at him. The guard resolved himself to the inevitable and dropped his weapon.

The two men, driver and guard, climbed from the top of the coach without a word.

"Drop them gun belts!" Smitty yelled at them. "You'd best move real careful like mister, I'm already halfway to gut shootin' ya!" His anger had not quite subsided. They did as they were told. Dropping their weapons like they were casting off a surrendered hope.

Smitty stepped to the driver and eyed him menacingly. "You about pulled my arm outta socket!" He complained.

The driver sneered at him. "It's just as easy to hang a one-armed man as it is a man with both!" He spit a stream of tobacco juice into Smitty's face and laughed!

Smitty stepped back. Rage and tobacco spit burned in his eyes! He cursed loudly through clenched teeth and leveled his pistol at the driver's face. Slate quickly swung his pistol over and shot the man in the foot.

The driver yelled in pain, falling to the ground. Smitty blinked his eyes, startled at the sudden interruption of his actions. He swept his own gun down on the man as he writhed in agony on the ground.

"That boy just saved your life, you stupid sumbitch!" He plucked the man's tobacco plug from his shirt pocket and knelt beside him, fury welling over him. "Open your mouth!" The man clenched his teeth. Smitty whacked him on the brow with the heel of his gun. "Open your damn mouth!" The driver squirmed with the pain. Smitty grabbed his jaw and forcefully crammed the entire plug into his mouth and held it closed. The man choked and gasped.

"There! You wanna spit, you rotten bastard, spit with that!" Smitty stood and kicked him viciously in the gut!

One of the women screamed. The driver curled up in a ball gagging on a mouthful of tobacco. His foot bled profusely. He groaned heavily.

The guard made a move to interfere but halted when the bore of Smitty's gun pressed hard against his forehead.

"I'll put you down good and permanent!" He hissed at him. Smitty stepped back and eyed the passengers. Their faces were masks of horror and fear. He motioned for Heck to go on up the hill and watch their back trail.

They had climbed out, one by one. Slate grabbed the men and shoved them to the side, Deke following them with his gun.

The two men were dressed in broadcloth suits. One sported a great handlebar mustache, the other a goatee with streaks of gray showing in it.

As the women exited, Slate merely motioned with the barrel of his pistol. The first woman clasped the arm of the man with the goatee, the other two clutched her and each other.

"See here! You'll not put your hands on these ladies!" the man exclaimed. Slate glared at him with narrowed eyes but said nothing.

The driver still lay sprawled on the ground writhing and cursing in pain. The guard went to help him, but froze when Smitty threatened to cave his skull in. "Let that dumb sumbitch waller on the ground and be glad he's not going under it!"

Smitty took a deep breath and let it out slowly. He shifted his eyes and scanned the people standing next to the stage. "Now folks. Since we got off on a... bad foot... let's see if we can salvage some degree of civility..."

He was trying to talk in a moderate tone. Slate was amazed at the uncharacteristic eloquence coming from the dusty old outlaw. "Just keep your hands up and don't move. My associates will come to you and you will remove your valuables and place them in their pokes. We ain't gonna hurt nobody else unless you force it on yourselves like this dumb sumbitch here did!"

Slate moved to the two men and swatted their coats open. He removed their wallets, watches and a cigar case. The man with the goatee had a fine hickory pipe and an oil skin full of tobacco.

When they came to the women, they merely motioned for them to comply. Deke stepped before them pointing at their jewelry as they removed it.

He came to the third one. She looked to be about his age. She had bright blue eyes that were at this time wide in terror. She wore a scarf over her hair, but there were wisps and curls of blonde hair emerging from the cover. He stood motionless for a moment looking into her eyes. She returned his gaze, trying not to shrink away. Her face was a picture of an angel, he thought. Fair complexion save for the pale of fear. She raised her hands to unfasten her necklace, but he shook his head. Her hands slowly lowered. He wanted to speak but thought better of it. On impulse he raised his hand and touched her hair.

"Get away from her!" The man with the mustache yelled. Deke's head snapped to the left. He scowled and stepped deliberately to the man, gun raised.

"No don't!" the girl shouted. "Please don't..." She pleaded.

Deke stopped in his tracks. He turned to face her again. She looked at him with a trembling lip, pleading with her eyes. A tear flowed down her cheek. Deke reached up and wiped it away. She fought the urge to recoil from his touch. He realized then, he was the reason for her terror and stepped back and away from her. He lowered his gun and his eyes.

Smitty ordered the guard and the man with the mustache to drop the box from behind the seat and pull the passengers bags down. He pointed at the men. "Open yours up." They did so grudgingly. They carried nothing of any importance or value.

The express box had a heavy lock on it. "Where's the key for that there box?" Smitty asked with a warning tone.

The guard answered. "It's in my pocket."

He looked over at him. "Well, shuck it out boy! Matter of fact empty your pockets in my friend's bag there!"

The guard hesitated.

"Oh, please just do it!" insisted the older woman. He did as he was told. Smitty grabbed the key and tossed it to Slate.

"Now empty your friend's pockets!" The guard hesitated again. Smitty stepped forward threateningly.

The woman again cried out. "Please, mister, do as he says!"

He rustled around in the driver's pockets though the wounded man hollered out in pain and protest. He deposited the items in Deke's bag and stood up straight.

"There now..." Smitty smirked. "That wasn't so hard, was it?" The man simply turned his head away.

Slate worked the key in the lock and yanked it open. There were four sacks marked 'First National Bank' inside. They appeared to be full of money. Slate's eyes grew wide and he struggled to not shout.

Smitty stepped back and motioned the others to do the same. He spoke to the passengers in a low voice. "Ya'll get them bags over to the side of the road. Drag that dumb sumbitch with you." He said pointing at the wounded driver.

When the task had been completed he removed a lantern from the side of the coach, opened it and dumped the contents into the stage. He pointed to the guard. "Unhitch that team and be quick about it!"

Once the horses were free, Smitty stepped to the coach, lit a match and tossed it inside! The oil burned quickly, spreading the flames throughout the coach, it was enveloped in a matter of minutes with a great "Swoosh!" It startled the hitch team. They bucked and galloped off kicking clods of dirt up behind them.

Deke watched the fire swallow up the stage. The flames reflected in his eyes. A haunting image came over him then, and he felt the pangs of loss. He looked again at the girl who clung to the other women. He felt lower than he ever had before. Even the weight of the gun in his hand was no comfort.

There was a tug on his shirt. It was Slate. He spoke in a low voice, but with urgency. "What're ya waitin' on? Let's go!"

Deke's eye swept the people quickly once again. His gaze met that of the girl and held it for the space of few heart beats. He solemnly tipped his hat and took his leave.

Smitty swept up the driver's and guard's weapons. "Ya'll better git on back around that bend there! Things are about to go from bad to worse!"

The passengers hurried out of the way of the impending danger. The guard helped the driver up, limping behind the others. "You'd better be glad I didn't stuff you in that coach before I set it on fire!" He hollered at the driver, then tossed the gun belts and shotgun into the burning stage.

The gang raced away. The sounds of bullets in the fire popped sporadically behind them.

They rode for a solid two hours. Slate whooped exuberantly. Deke clutched his reins and felt something heavy he didn't recognize in his gut.

They gathered by a stream that ran next to a mountain. A thick cover of brush concealed the camp.

The sacks were dumped on a horse blanket as before. Slate opted for the fine hickory pipe and tobacco. The bank satchels were inspected. Each held one thousand dollars. They split the money up into their individual saddle bags, which were now growing heavy.

Smitty's face was still a mask of anger, but the sight of all that money brightened him up a good bit.

"You sure raised hell today! You was gonna kill that man." Slate said to him.

Smitty's jaw was set tight. "You're damned right I was!" He spat. "Half tempted to ride back there and do it anyway..."

"Well, he'll have to hold all his dance cards for a while." Heck grinned. The others looked at him like he had just figured out the answer to a puzzle. They finally laughed.

"That old boy can count his lucky stars tonight." Smitty added.

They divvied up the rest of the loot. Heck grabbed the driver's pocket knife.

"I kind of figured you wasn't gonna let them boys alone." Slate mentioned referring to the driver and guard being relieved of their valuables.

"Nope!" Smitty replied. "I still say they're lucky they got away with their skins."

Slate was thoughtful for a moment. "Ya know, you're a talker, Smitty. You an educated man?"

The old man smiled crooked, speaking in a low tone like he was telling a secret. "I went to a university once when I was a young man."

The boys looked surprised. Understandably so. They only knew him as a grizzled old coot who collected bad habits and had a mean streak so wide a cougar wouldn't cross it.

"I didn't stay though..." He admitted.

"What made ya quit?" Heck asked.

"Didn't quit. Got throwed out."

"What for?"

"I beat the snot out of a smart aleck professor."

"Sounds about right." Slate exclaimed.

Deke sat alone. The money, cigars and whiskey didn't interest him. All he could see were the blue eyes of the girl. He could still feel the softness of her hair and the gracefulness of her cheek. He was morose and convoluted in his thoughts. *'What kind of girl is she...?'* he thought.

"Deke. Deke!" Slate called.

Deke lifted his head, turning his face to where the others sat.

"Where ya at boy? Come on over here." Slate invited.

Heck laughed a little. "He's all wadded up about that pretty little gal." He chuckled.

Deke's eyes narrowed and he looked toward Heck with a grim expression.

"I seen that gal." Heck smiled. "Yup, she sure was a sweet plum ripe for the pickin'!"

Deke lunged at Heck's throat. Heck stepped back untouched as Slate bolted in between the two. "Hold on there Deke! There won't be none of that!"

Deke sneered at Heck who still held his smile.

"Ah hell, I was just joshin', boy!" Heck stated.

Deke jerked himself away and skulked off to stand by a tree. He gazed at the stars, just coming into view. He was angry and embarrassed. The heavy thing in his gut still sat there. His thinking was getting mixed up.

Slate walked over to him and placed a hand on his shoulder. Deke shucked it away. "Calm down. Heck was just joshin with ya." He said.

"He's lucky you was there..." Deke spat.

"You don't want to tangle with Heck Braden. No you don't!" Slate warned. "He's a nice fella, it takes a lot to get him mad; but if you do, you'll damn sure wish you hadn't. He's a bad one when he gets on the wrong side of his temper."

Deke stood tall and thrust out his chest. "You might say the same about me!" He insisted. "Folks might oughta be a little more careful about gettin' on the wrong side of me!" He wanted to strike out, to hurt something or someone.

Slate considered it. "Yup. You're right. I just might. But Deke, that ain't a good thing to have to say about a man, any man."

Slate walked back to where the others were. Sat down and lit his fine new hickory pipe.

CHAPTER EIGHT

Bill paced back and forth. He was anxious and on edge. "Where the hell is Bobby?!" He asked.

Thomas and Charlie shrugged, shaking their heads.

Presently the man in question emerged into the camp. "Where the hell you been?!" Bill insisted.

Bobby sat down and dusted off his sleeves. He took a long drink from a canteen then set it down forcefully. "It don't look good, Bill. There's soldiers all over the place down there and I think I even saw a U.S. Marshal."

Bill clenched his teeth and kicked at the dust. "I didn't see anything much better on my end either." He growled.

The two men had been scouting the stage stations between El Rico and Santa Paula. That the government had taken an interest into their activities was quite apparent.

"How about our back trail?" Thomas queried.

Bill looked at him but said nothing.

"What ya wanna do?" Bobby asked.

"I reckon we'd better lay low for a while. Let's slip on out of here and find us some friendlier territory."

That was just the news the others were hoping for. They gathered their gear and did what they could to mask the evidence of their having been there. They walked their horses for a good long way. Far enough, Bill thought, that any dust they might stir would not be seen.

"We oughta stash this loot, Bill." Charlie said.

"We will, once we get to where we're goin."

They rode easy throughout the day, making a cold camp that night. Another day of travel brought them to a low-lying building on an ill-defined road. It was constructed half of sod and half of rough-hewn lumber. It appeared to have crawled up out of the ground, hunkered down, and stayed there.

A thin trail of smoke emanated from a crooked stove pipe in the roof.

They sat their horses and watched the place for a long time. They saw a man walking out the front door, stepping to the side of the building and relieving himself on the wall. He buttoned up and went quickly back inside.

"What is this place?" Thomas asked.

Bill rubbed his whiskers and spit next to horses left hoof. "I ain't never been really sure." He said.

The others exchanged curious glances.

"You stay here. Matter of fact, back off a might." Bill instructed taking up his rein. "I'll be back. If I ain't, you'll hear the shootin' then come a runnin'."

Bill ambled his horse on toward the building. His eyes sweeping the area cautiously. He removed the rawhide from the hammer of his sidearm and loosened the weapon in its holster.

There were a couple of rangy horses that looked like they hadn't been ridden in a while in the corral. They were gaunt and shabby creatures, more suited to slaughter than anything else.

He sat his saddle in front of the place, looking it over. It hadn't changed much since the last time he was there, at least from what he could tell from the outside.

He stepped down and tied his mount to the rail, hitched up his britches, settled his gun belt, walked up three wide steps to the porch, twisted the knob and walked inside.

It was dark inside the place. The windows on either side of the room only allowed angled shafts of dim light through their dirt smudged panes. Dust particles whirled around and floated in the light.

A man sat at a bar. He wore checkered pants and old shoes with run down heels, a jacket of sorts, with frayed hems, and a dented bowler hat. He had a scruffy beard of several day's growth. His clothes looked like he'd slept in them. The man had the appearance of one who had blown in one day, sat there and never got back up. He twisted his neck and eyed Bill up and down with no particular expression.

Bill's eyes adjusted to the interior quickly. He walked to the bar without acknowledging the stranger, inspecting the doorways and behind the bar. Nothing or anyone stirred.

"Who ya lookin' for?" the stranger asked.

Bill didn't reply.

"I said, who ya lookin for?!" the stranger repeated in a louder voice.

Bill's knuckles turned white. "Say one more word to me and I'll cut your tongue out."

The stranger shrank away, picked up his drink and moved to a table in the corner.

Then Bill saw movement in the back room. The smell of frying bacon and potatoes wafted into the room. "Who's out there, Coy?" came a gravely woman's voice.

The stranger hesitated to speak, watching Bill cautiously as he did so. "I don't know. Some fella…"

Bill knew the voice and he relaxed. The woman with the gravelly voice emerged from the back, wiping her hands on an old coarse towel. She hesitated a moment when she saw the big outlaw standing there. She lowered her head, squinted her eyes, and studied the face of the man standing at the bar. She threw her arms up and laughed! "Well, I declare!"

Bill blushed under his beard and smiled. "Howdy, Ma!"

She sped around the bar and threw her arms around him. "Bill where have you been, son?" She stepped back and studied him. "I swear you're skinny as a rail! Hadn't you been eatin' good?"

"Well, I been out on the trail lately and I…"

She cut him off. "You sit yourself down boy and have some food."

Bill shrugged away as politely as he was capable of. "I got some boys up in the hills. I need to go fetch 'em. You got enough for all of us?"

She placed her hands on her hips. "Course I do. Go get your friends and bring 'em on in."

Bill nodded and strolled to the door, scowling at Coy as he passed.

Riding up to the others, he knew there would be confusion and questions coming, but decided to take it as it came about. He hated to share this place, but necessity required it.

"Come on, boys, there's grub a waitin'."

They didn't hesitate. They rode to the place at a rapid trot. Instead of tying their horses off at the rail, Bill directed to put them in the corral and strip their saddles. "Bring your bags in."

They did as instructed. Once inside they sat at a large round table. The woman smiled sweetly at them all. She was missing her front teeth. She fussed over them as though they were the returned prodigals. She set plates around the table and piled them up with potatoes and bacon. There was fresh made bread and plenty of coffee.

She stopped at Bill's chair and hugged him. He tried to lean away, but there was no escape. "I sure am glad to see you, son!"

Bobby dropped his fork. The three men looked at Bill as if they'd never saw him before.

Coy called from over at the corner table. "Ma, you got any more of this lemonade?"

Charlie quickly put and two and two together and came up with the idea Coy was Bill's brother.

"Is that your brother?" He asked in a low voice.

Bill had a mouthful of food. He gulped it down and swallowed it with half a cup of coffee. "Hell no, that ain't my brother!" He grumbled. "I never seen him before."

The three men looked perplexed.

"Just eat your damn food!" Bill barked.

The woman walked around the table as they ate. "My, you boys was about half starved." she said, admiring their wolfish appetites. "Bill, you haven't even introduced your friends."

Bill wiped his mouth and pointed them out hurriedly. That there is Bobby. That there is Charlie, and that there is Thomas."

The men nodded as they were indicated.

"Boys, this here is Ma."

"Ma?'

"Yup, Ma."

"Your Ma?"

Bill gritted his teeth. "No. Just Ma."

She stood proudly and smiled at them like they were her own children. She raised her hand to her cheek with a red flush to her face, turning to glance at Coy. "Have you met Coy?" she asked.

Coy stood, smoothing his pants legs. "We've, uh, not been properly introduced." He said meekly.

She motioned him over and put her arm around him. "This is Coy, He's my husband."

It was Bill's turn to drop his fork. "Husband?"

"Yup! Coy come in here a few months ago. He didn't have nowheres to go. Couple days later, a circuit preacher come through and asked if we was husband and wife." She giggled coarsely through the story. "Of course, we weren't and we didn't have nothin' better to do, so we just hauled off and got ourselves hitched!"

She grinned at Coy, he smiled the best he could. Coy stuck out his hand. "Pleased to meet ya, Bill."

Bill glared at the hand wanting to bite it off. Ma nudged him insistently. He reached out and shook Coy's hand in the manner a man might draw a dead snake out of a cesspool.

Ma beamed again at her company. "It's so nice to have you boys here at home!"

The men exchanged another round of curious expressions.

Bill considered the saddle bags. "We've got some things we'd like to hold here, if it's alright, Ma." He said

"Why, sure, of course, son. You know where they go." Bill stood up with his saddle bag. The others did the same. He motioned with his head for them to follow him."

Coy stepped up eagerly. "Can I help in any way?" Four sets of eyes bore through him until he stepped aside.

Down a narrow hallway, there was an old chest that appeared to have been built into the structure. Bill pushed on a hidden lever and lifted the old trunk out of the way. A compartment of sorts opened beneath it. "Well I'll be damned." Thomas exclaimed. They placed the bags inside.

Bill reached in his and withdrew a small gold bar and a long necklace. They replaced the chest and Bill reset the hidden lever. "Ma's second or third husband built that." He explained. That old boy was mighty handy.

"Whatever become of him? Bobby asked.

"He got hung for stealin' horses and killin' a couple fellas." Bill replied.

When they re-entered the room Coy sat back in a chair smoking a cigarette. Ma sat with him in an old rocker. Bill handed her the gold bar and necklace. "This is for you." She gasped in appreciation.

"Oh my!" she exclaimed. She stood and put the necklace on, turning to and fro showing it off. She stepped to an old dusty mirror and admired it on herself. "You shouldn't have, Bill! That's so nice!" She hugged him again and kissed him on the cheek.

Bobby thought he would choke. Bill scowled at them. His glare held a dire warning that didn't need words.

"You boys bed down in back whenever you're ready. I'm sure you must be tired." They were.

Coy ambled around the bar. "Ya'll want a drink of some fine whiskey?" The boys agreed to that on the spot. They drank sparingly, however, because Bill told them to.

Soon Coy left the room. Bobby peeked after him to see if he'd gone out of earshot.

He looked at Bill, estimated the space between them and decided it was safe enough.

"Charlie thought that fella was your brother. Turns out he's your step-daddy!"

Bill growled and reached for Bobby's throat, but he wasn't fast enough. The others snickered in their drinks. "I'm gonna kick the daylights out of you one of these days!"

The next day they rustled around and tended their stock. They planned on holding up there for a while, at least a few days.

Coy came out and fussed around the two soapy horses.

"Them your animals?" Charlie asked.

Coy made like he was more horseman than he was. "Yup. Good mounts these two..." Charlie looked them over shaking his head. Thomas moseyed over and did the same. Bill looked over like he'd just bit something sour.

"They're for sale if you're interested." Coy offered eagerly.

Thomas scoffed. "How much you want for 'em?"

"Oh, I don't know... These are good horses, just need some good feed is all."

Charlie plucked two cartridges from his gun belt and held them in his palm.

"That's about all their worth right there."

The boys played cards and passed the time repairing bridles and gear. Bobby noticed a newspaper folded up on a table. Picking it up, he read the headline out loud. "Murder and Brutality!"

As he read the story out loud, Bill's expression grew darker with every sentence. When he read the part about the territorial senator's murdered son-in-law, an audible groan emanated from the others.

"That explains a lot." Bobby offered. "You reckon Carl's seen this?"

Bill nodded. "Yup."

Coy had been sitting unnoticed. "You cain't trust them damn reporters!"

No one acknowledged his statement. Bill huffed loudly when he heard the report regarding the 'citizen host'. He shook his head.

"See that's the trick right there." Thomas explained. "You can be a low-life snake but get yourself killed by being stupid and all of a sudden you're an upstanding member of society." He shook his head. "Reckon I'll have to remember that."

Nightfall came with a bright moon shining overhead. The place was silent save for the snores of its occupants. A lone figure eased across the front room, gathered some things up and slipped out the door. He walked quickly, but quietly around the house and into the coral. Taking a saddle and bridle from the racks, he began outfitting Bill Sinclair's horse.

The sound of the hammer cocking on a Colt .44 stopped him in his tracks.

He turned slowly, frightfully seeking out the location of the sound. The form of Bill Sinclair emerged from the shadows and into the moonlight. Coy swallowed hard, a cold, bony finger traced his spine.

"That's my horse." Bill stated flatly.

Coy tried to make out like he'd made a mistake. He quickly busied himself with removing the tack from the animal.

Bill took another step forward. "That's Thomas' saddle."

Coy's shoulders slumped as he gave up. He knew he was caught and nothing he could say would save him. He replaced the items back where he'd found them.

Bill said nothing else but took another step forward and held out his hand.

Coy looked at him innocently. "Wh-What...?" He stammered.

Bill stepped forward again, a sinister scowl darkened his features. That he wanted to punish this man with vile severity was evident. His eyes flared when Coy pretended innocence.

"You know damn good and well what." His hand was still extended.

Coy lowered his head and reached in his pockets. He withdrew the gold bar and necklace Bill had given Ma and placed them in Bill's hand.

"Are-Are you going to k-kill me now?"

"Why shouldn't I?" He growled. "You know what you are. What good are you?"

Coy was nearly in tears. "Please, I made a mistake. Let me go. I can't stay here."

Bill's anger never wavered. "It was good enough when you were draggin' your sorry carcass with nothin' but the teeth in your mouth."

Coy nodded. "Y-You're right. But, mister, I can't do it. I just can't. That woman's gonna kill me. I just cain't keep up."

Bill looked as if he'd just swallowed a gnat. He stepped forward again, close enough to rest the muzzle of his pistol against the bridge of Coy's nose. "Looks like you get to choose..."

Coy put his trembling hands in the air. "Okay, okay... Let's just forget about it, okay?"

Bill shook his head. "Nope. I'll be keeping an eye on you. I ever see you anywhere but right here keeping Ma happy; I'll gut and skin you like the no-good varmint you are."

Coy's lip trembled and his knees wobbled. He nodded deeply. Bill placed the items back in Coy's hand. "These things better be right back where you got 'em." Coy nodded again and slowly walked back inside. Bill spat disdainfully after him.

The following day, the men sat about passing the time when the door opened, and Raymond walked in, his face dirt streaked. He appeared to have been riding hard. He stopped inside the door and looked around. The other men saw him and called him over. He acknowledged them but walked straight to Bill who was leaned back in a stuffed chair. "The boss told me to give you this."

Bill looked at it and plucked a pair of spectacles from his pocket. "You read this?" He asked Raymond.

"No, sir. Hell, no!" He responded.

Bill nodded and waved him away. He joined the others receiving slaps on the back and eager handshakes. "What is this place?" He asked looking around.

"We ain't never been sure." Bobby replied.

CHAPTER NINE

Carl sat, propped up on his bed, hands folded behind his head. His boots lay on the floor where he kicked them off. Cotton leaned back in a chair reading the newspaper. Carl frowned and studied the wall.

"Savage gang led by a madman. Stagecoach burned to cinders!" Cotton read aloud, then added. "Slate must be letting Smitty take the lead on the jobs."

He read further, "Thirty-year veteran teamster grievously wounded and savagely beaten by the leader of the gang after courageously defying their demands!"

Carl snickered. "That'll show him to buck old Smitty!"

Cotton agreed. "Did you know he was a educated man? Smitty, I mean."

Carl pursed his lips. "Yup heard he went to some fancy college back east. Killed the principle or somethin'"

"I heard he shot the dean of the school and run off with his wife..." Cotton commented.

A thoughtful silence followed. "Reckon we'll have to remember to ask him one of these days." Cotton added.

A knock sounded on the door.

"Yeah!" Carl hollered.

The door swung open slowly and Pedro's head poked in. "You wanted to see us boss?"

"Come on in, Pedro."

Pedro entered, Raymond followed behind him. Carl sat up and moved to a writing desk that was situated in the corner of the room.

He picked up two notes and handed them to each man. They were sealed.

"I want you boys to go find Bill, and Slate. Give them these papers."

The two looked at each other, then at the notes in their hands and shrugged. "Where are they?" Raymond asked.

Carl pulled some more papers out of the desk drawer and began sketching out rough maps for where the men should be found.

He passed one to Pedro. "You go up to that road. Ride up and down it until they find you."

Pedro nodded. "What if they don't find me?" He asked.

"Then there won't be any reason to give 'em those notes." Cotton offered.

He handed the second map to Raymond. "There's a place out there you'll find, if you follow this trail. I imagine Bill will likely be there."

Raymond eyed the map curiously. "What kind of place is it?"

Carl pondered a moment. "I ain't never been sure..."

The two men left the hotel, walked to the livery and saddled their horses. Pedro noticed a man leaning on the corner of a building across the street watching them. He was one of Molina's men. "I'll be glad to be gone from this place." He whispered to Raymond.

Raymond eyed the man. "Me too. Watch your back trail."

They shook hands briefly and rode off. The hair on Pedro's neck didn't lay back down until he had many miles behind him.

Cotton peered out the window. "Yup. He's there alright..." He watched Pedro and Raymond ride off. The vaquero by the building watched them also.

Carl pulled on his boots, and his vest, buckled his gun belt on, and placed his hat on his head. "Let's go see Señor Molina."

The men strode over to the cantina where Miguel and his men had rooms.

When Carl and Cotton entered, the bartender held his hand up. "Go no farther, Gringo!" There was only a half dozen men in the room. They turned to eye the men who the bartender spoke to. Three Molina vaqueros sat at a table. One stood and walked up the steps in the back of the room. Another spoke to the bartender in a harsh tone.

The man changed his demeanor like someone trying on hats. The one he settled on didn't fit him any better than the rest.

Miguel Molina walked down the stairs, Juan was close behind. He nodded at Carl and Cotton. "Forgive my rude friend." He said. Then faced the bartender. "Julio! These men are our allies! You'll show them the proper respect!"

The bartender nodded deeply. "Si, Señor. My apologies."

"We have to be very careful here, Señor Ferguson. Surely you understand."

Carl nodded to the affirmative. Cotton swept his gaze over the room. That those men were fighters was apparent. If he'd had to go for his gun, he figured the best he could would be to try to empty it before he died. He didn't much like the situation.

"Let's meet at the hotel cafe." He suggested. "There's a back room there where we can talk in private."

Miguel looked around him. "You don't like it here?" He asked.

"No." Carl and Cotton said in unison.

"Very well. It is no problem." Miguel agreed. "Juan and I will meet you there in an hour."

"In an hour." Carl said.

Miguel turned toward the stairs. He scowled at the bartender as he passed him.

When they were gathered at a table Carl tapped his finger deliberately. "Why do have you a man watching us?" He demanded.

Miguel was taken aback. He looked at his brother then back to Carl and Cotton. He shrugged his shoulders. "I don't have anyone watching you." He said.

Carl leaned back. "Ain't you the one who said something about talking plain?"

Miguel nodded. "Yes. Yes, I did. I assure you. I have no-one watching you."

Cotton piped in. "Well then, somebody in your camp is up to something you don't know about."

Miguel sat back and studied the thought. He drummed his fingers on the table. "My men are loyal, Señor Cotton." He said it as if he wasn't completely convinced of the statement himself.

He leaned over to Juan who spoke softly to him. Miguel's face grew sullen. "Okay." He said to his brother, patting him on the shoulder as he rose to leave.

"We have had an occasion or two when my uncle has placed one of his men into our company to spy on us. I know he does this because I have caught them. We do the same thing. It goes very badly for those who are caught..." Miguel's face had grown darker. "My brother is looking into something he has suspected for a while. We will hear back from him presently."

Carl leaned back in his chair. "Hey, Cotton, you reckon that lady in the kitchen has some coffee?" Cotton nodded. "I imagine..." Carl smiled but said nothing. Cotton got up and went to the kitchen.

"I don't know what you have planned, Miguel, I understand your situation. Hell, I admire you for it. But, I ain't real excited about tangling up in another man's war."

Miguel nodded his head. "I understand. What I have in mind will not cause you to do so, not directly. I think you can help a great deal by simply doing what you and your men do best."

Cotton sauntered back into the room and took his chair. Behind him a lady brought a pot of coffee on a tray with four cups, the same too-small porcelain cups.

Miguel withdrew a map from inside his jacket and spread it out on the table. It showed their present location and the entire north and west area. Carl noted his ranch was marked on it as well, causing him to raise an eyebrow in question.

"It seems your diversions have had a good effect." He said. "I have learned the American Federales and the Marshals are not interested any longer in greeting our silver at the border. My uncle is a powerful man. He has bribed many in high offices. I expect there to be something of a presence of men from these offices."

"If you tie up with the Army or the law, they'll be down on you like a ton of bricks." Carl said.

Miguel agreed. "I am hoping we won't have to. I also have bribed many in high places."

"It gets pretty thick don't it?" Cotton offered.

Miguel nodded. "Yes, it does. Yes, it does..."

Carl studied the map, working out where and how would be the best place to seize the silver wagon and what to do with it afterward. "I imagine you'll get a hold it before it crosses the river." He said.

"That's right. I have influence in the Mexican Federales. The commander of the company that is supposed to deliver it is a good friend. He knows my uncle and hates him almost as much as I do! I still need to get it across however. We will use our mules to pack it instead of a wagon and cross the Gila Mountains to my hacienda. We have boats to carry it across the river."

Carl could see the lay of the land and appreciated Miguel's ingenuity. "I don't see why you need us in this plan." He said.

Miguel's finger landed on the Molina Rancho marked on the map. He traced the roads leading out to their location. "My uncle will send a company of his men to take possession of the silver. They will travel one or maybe even both of these roads."

The idea was becoming a little clearer. Cotton stuck his lip out, leaning on the table as he studied Miguel's plan. "You want us to hold them up so you have time to get the silver and get away?"

Miguel nodded again. "That's right. Maybe not engage in a battle but harass them. Steal their horses, guns, supplies. Hell, I don't care if you take their women! Whatever you take, you are welcome to keep." His face grew serious. "Don't underestimate Raul's men, amigo. This will not be easy. I promise, you will lose some men. Maybe even all of them if you are too careless. They are fighters, and many have vowed their lives to my uncle's service."

"When do you expect those men to head this way?"

Miguel thought a minute. "I think in about five or six days according to my information. It could be more or less, but not by much. You will know them when you see them. They will travel as an army would. They wear yellow sashes around their waists. Their horses are very fine, and they eat only the best food. They will place many guards on their camps.

At first however, they might not expect any trouble, which could be in your favor."

Carl leaned back in his chair. "Looks like a hell of a fix. You still haven't said what we're gonna get out of it. If me and my men are going to tangle up in your war, you gotta make it worth our while."

"I know." Miguel said. "And I will. I have a chest that is my personal chest. It has enough to make one man wealthy beyond his imagination, or many men wealthy enough to make them very happy."

"Where's this chest at?" Cotton asked.

"I have it. I will give it to you once I am at my hacienda with my silver. Until then, I have gold to offer as a good faith gesture."

Carl considered the plan. He knew well, that most men had a bad habit of underestimating their opposition. He took what Miguel had said about his uncle's men and doubled it. But he could see a way, a few ways as a matter of fact, to make it work.

"Alright. We'll do it." He stood and offered his hand. Miguel grinned, leapt to his feet and grasped Carl's hand shaking it vigorously.

"I will contact you tonight, for the gold. I think there might also be something else you might be interested in."

With that, Miguel Molina strode out of the hotel. Carl and Cotton sat back down and had a cup of coffee. "What ya think, boss?" Cotton asked.

Carl sipped his coffee. "We'll see. We'll see..."

Carl sat at the writing desk in his room. He was redrawing the maps Miguel showed from memory. He added familiar landmarks, natural barriers, and trails that weren't on the original map. He outlined probable campsites and avenues of approach to them.

A light knock brought him from his work. He placed his hand on his gun and turned to face the door.

"Yeah!" He called.

A voice with a Spanish accent came from the other side. "Señor. Señor Molina wishes to see you and Señor Cotton at the grain barn."

He heard footsteps retreat.

They approached the barn cautiously. A large building constructed of wide planks, it stood on the edge of the town, separated from other buildings. There was a loft with a hoist that hung from the front. They came to the door from either side. One side of the large doors was open about a foot. Cotton peered inside. A group of vaqueros were standing in a semicircle in the middle. Their backs were to him. Lantern light shown in the middle of the group, he heard angry voices and a pained scream coming from within. He motioned to Carl and they eased inside.

The vaqueros turned. Their faces mostly shadowed by their wide sombreros.

Juan stepped out and motioned them forward.

The man they saw watching Pedro and Raymond was tied to a post in the middle. His shirt was torn away from him. Great purple bruises and lacerations shown on his chest and ribs. His face was swollen and bloody. One of his legs looked as if it had been broken.

Miguel pointed at the man. "Is this the peon you saw watching?" He asked.

Carl eyed the man and nodded. The man was difficult to recognize in his current state, but Carl knew it was the same individual. "That's the one." He answered.

Miguel slapped the man hard! "Peon! You shame yourself and your family!"

Juan stood with Carl and Cotton. "He is a traitor. He has been caught spying. He will pay the price."

The man sobbed and cursed. He called out in pain as the men in the circle took turns striking him.

"What information have you told Raul?!" The man shook his head. Again, they struck him. The man winced and strained at the beating. Still, he remained silent save for his oaths and tears.

He looked up and glared at Carl and angrily spat blood and broken teeth toward him. "You will die, gringo! All of you will die!" He laughed a hysterical laugh. Carl drew his gun with a sneer.

"Wait, amigo." Miguel insisted. "That is too easy for this worm."

Juan stepped to the man and withdrew his long thin knife. The man screamed and squirmed. Two men held him in place. Juan grasped the man's chin in a brutal grip and glared into his eyes. "My face is the last thing you will see!"

He cut the man's ears off, and dropped them in a box, he jabbed the tip of his knife into his eye sockets and twisted the blade savagely removing the man's eyes. The man screamed with all he had within him, a high pitched primeval scream that emanated from the core of his being. He squirmed, crying out, desperately kicking his legs in torment. The two others held him so tightly against the post that his feet came off the floor. Bones cracked in his shoulders. Juan dropped the man's eyes into the box, shaking the blood and sinew from his fingers.

Miguel removed a sword and scabbard from a blue velvet case. "This was my father's and his fathers before him, and his before him. Now it is mine." It was a beautiful weapon. The scabbard was adorned with graceful etching, gold, silver, and rubies. A large 'M' with a gold cross adorned it. It was a weapon forged in an ancient Spaniard fire generations before.

Miguel drew the sword from the scabbard, admiring it with wide, malicious eyes. He approached the man. Lamp light played off the glimmering blade and emblazoned hilt. He raised the weapon and slashed the man open from the center of his chest to his groin. His entrails fell out and spilled onto the ground at his feet.

The man cried out in agony! "K-Kill me!" He pleaded. "K-Kill me!" He begged. "k-kill me..." He said again, in a barely audible voice.

Juan viciously pulled the man's tongue out and sliced it off, placing it in the box as well. The man made a gurgling sound that came from deep down within him. The others released him letting him sag in place, blood streaming from his wounds.

"Raul sent him here to be his eyes and ears and to tell what he has seen and heard. We will make sure

Raul gets what he wishes!" The man emitted a guttural, animal like sound and died.

"My gawd." Cotton exclaimed quietly. "My gawd..." His face had turned pale and he felt like he might be sick. The ruined body of the man, caught as a spy for Raul, sagged pathetically from the bindings like an old sack of wet grain.

Miguel cleaned the blade on a shred of the man's clothing and replaced it in the scabbard, then returned it to its velvet case. He produced several bottles of tequila and shouted exuberantly. "AAAIIIEEEEE!" The others joined in and drank as though they were celebrating a wedding. He offered a bottle to Carl and Cotton. The later grabbed it and chugged a great, repetitive swallow.

"You boys sure know how to hurt a man." He said.

Miguel had a leather sack in each hand. He handed one to Carl and one to Cotton. The two men bounced them in their hands, the sound of large heavy coins made them smile. "This is only a small part." He said, grinning. He raised his bottle. "To a long and prosperous alliance!"

The men drank deeply.

Tracy T. Thurman

CHAPTER TEN

Heck walked his horse into the camp. "Look who I found!" Pedro followed him in. He looked tired and hungry.

Slate stood from where he was. "What's going on, Pedro?"

The man shook his head and handed him the note Carl instructed him to deliver. "I don't know what's going on, but it's not good." He said.

Slate unfolded the paper and read quickly. "Alright boys. We're headed back to the ranch."

They gathered their gear, saddled their horses and rode out.

"We'd better take a different trail." Heck stated.

"That's what we'll do." Slate agreed.

Deke rode second in line behind Slate, then Smitty, with Pedro bringing up the rear. The trail was hilly and rocky; tree branches extended into their path, causing them to duck or push them out of the way.

Deke had to duck quickly to avoid a springy branch Slate had pushed aside. He looked back and saw Heck riding behind him. Heck seemed to be looking around at the scenery. Deke backed his mount off, adding a little more distance between himself and Slate. In so doing he effectively closed the gap between himself and Heck. Slate pushed another long branch out of the way. When it swung back sharply, Deke caught it, shoving it back as far he could reach, holding it until he passed. He let the branch slip. It sprung back with the force of an angry slap, whacking Heck across the face, knocking his hat off and nearly unsaddling him!

"What the hell'd you do that for?" Heck complained, as he stopped his horse and stepped down to retrieve his hat. Smitty cackled behind him doubled over in the saddle holding his gut. Pedro looked ahead at his predicament and laughed as well.

Deke turned and shrugged. "I was just joshin'..." He said innocently. He leaned forward and chuckled to himself. Heck stepped back aboard cussing, dabbing his hand against a scratch seeping blood on his cheek. Slate shook his head and rode on.

The following day, they turned off the trail onto a section of road that would lead them to the turn off to the Ferguson ranch. They were tired and saddle weary.

"I wonder if old Flap Jacks will have some grub on."

"I sure hope so. My stomach's startin, ta think my throat's been cut! Maybe Doralee will have some of that cobbler cooked up!" Smitty replied enthusiastically.

Bill sat at the long table cleaning his fingernails with a pocket knife.

I see you got the same note?" Slate prompted.

Bill simply nodded in reply but said nothing. Slate shrugged. *'Some things never change.'* he thought.

Carl stepped out of the house and strode to where Bill was sitting. He had rolled up papers in his hand.

"Howdy Slate. Glad ya made it back in one piece."

Slate swung from the saddle and handed his reins to Deke, who continued with the rest to the corral.

"We made some pretty strong impressions and got away with quite a poke of prizes." He said.

Carl nodded, twisting a twig in his teeth. "Yeah, I read about it in the newspapers. I'd say ya'll made an impression alright."

Bill grumbled something under his breath.

Carl slapped Slate on the back. "Get yourselves settled in and grab some grub. We'll have a meeting tonight at the house."

Flap Jacks grinned wide when the boys walked into the mess tent. "Well looky what the cat drug in Doralee! A bunch of skunks!"

Deke grinned at his friend. "I ain't no skunk! But it sure smells like one's been here!"

"Ha! If I smelled like you boys, I'd stay away from decent folk!"

Slate looked around curiously. "I ain't seen no decent folk here about, Flap Jacks."

Doralee smiled at them. "They ain't skunks, husband, they just need some food."

The men looked about hungrily. The smell of broiled beef coaxed them closer. Smitty licked his chops. There were beef steaks, biscuits and potatoes forked up in royal portions, even corn on the cob, Doralee had traded for some pies town. The men attacked the food like wolves.

Flap Jacks sat among them and listened to them talk with their mouths full about their recent excursion. As they were winding down on their first helpings, Doralee came in holding a Dutch oven using heavy cloths in each hand. She set it in the middle of the table and pulled off the lid.

The fragrance of the peach cobbler was a siren song, calling even Slate to the idea of maybe not having a second steak in order to save plenty of room for the cobbler. She laid a large wooden spoon across the top, then stepped back and smiled.

Deke reached for it, but Heck grabbed it first. Flicking his wrist, he whacked Deke sharply on the knuckles. Deke recoiled but didn't give up, grabbing the kettle and trying to slide it his way. Heck had a great scoop of the desert on the spoon and eagerly moved it through the air to his plate. Smitty quickly moved his own plate over Heck's and intercepted the portion as he dropped it. Heck placed his hands on the table glowering at the cobbler thief, giving Deke the opportunity to swipe the spoon from his hand. He dug into the pot and held his prize high. "Anybody want some? There's a plenty!" Heck tried to snatch it back, but Deke pulled it away.

"I'll take some of that!" Slate announced.

Deke dumped the cobbler on Slate's plate and dug in again. "Anybody else...?" He offered, still avoiding Heck's efforts to regain control of the spoon.

"I'll have some Deke!" Pedro reached his plate over receiving the next portion. Heck was cussing now and reached again. Deke swatted his knuckles just as Heck had done to him.

"Dammit boy, gimme that spoon!"

After Deke delivered a large portion to himself, he dropped the spoon in the nearly empty pot. "You can have all the rest Heck!" He said.

Heck grabbed the pot and gazed inside, then at the plates of the others. Disappointment, and a shade of envy, showed in his eyes. "Ya'll didn't leave much!" He complained. Smitty looked at him with an expression of sympathy. "It's a tough life bein' an outlaw…" Raucous laughter followed as Heck scraped the bottom of the Dutch oven.

Doralee, tucked under the arm of Flap Jacks, smiled widely and laughed.

"Them boys are plain crazy." Flap Jacks said.

Later that night. Carl spread the maps out on the table. Bill, Slate, Heck, and Cotton gazed at the maps and listened to Carl speak. He explained the meetings with Miguel Molina and the alliance they had agreed upon.

"Why didn't you figure this Molina deal before?" Bill asked impatiently.

Carl drew a deep breath and paused shifting his gaze to the big man. "Because the silver shipment was being done under secrecy. I only found out about it from a loose talking, drunk Mexican soldier. The Molina's didn't figure into it."

Carl despised having to explain himself but figured there was good cause to do so.

Bill pursed his lips and nodded. "I guess it was a gamble to start with. Looks like we'll draw different cards."

Carl explained, with Cotton's input, the whole fracas with the Molina Rancho and how this could turn out to be a good deal. He and Cotton dropped the leather bags Miguel had given them in the middle of the table and described the chest they were to receive after the dust settled.

"It won't take long. A few days, maybe a week. It ain't going to be easy though. The Molina's are an educated, military family. Their outfit reflects that in every way." Carl explained.

He glanced at the faces of the men around the table to make sure they fully understood. He saw some doubt there and expounded on his words. "What I'm saying is; these ain't no run of the mill folks. This ain't knocking over a stage or holdin' up a bank. These men are professionals and we need to remember that."

The men agreed. They each already forming tactical plans in their minds and which men they would take with them on whatever job they were given.

Carl traced the roads and direction of travel the Raul Molina's crew would likely take. He also described the plan Miguel had shared with him as to what his plans were.

"I have a strategy worked out, but it will take some luck and a whole lot of quick moving to make it work." Carl straightened himself and reached over for the coffee pot that was sitting on the stove and filled his cup. Bill scowled at the table and subconsciously shook his head. He hated when Carl would do that, stopping in the middle of something to do something else. Carl knew he hated it. That's why he did it.

"I want two teams of two men. Ride out to the west here, two good days of hard riding. Watch the roads at these points. Then haul ass back here."

He motioned to Cotton and Heck. "Pick a man to ride with you. Cotton take the south road; Heck, the north road. Pack light and travel fast. Get as much information as you can on their forces, equipment, weapons and supplies. I don't have to tell you not to get caught and don't be seen."

Cotton nodded with wide eyes. "Don't get caught!" He repeated.

Cotton then relayed the story of the night at the grain barn in Mescolare. He shuddered involuntarily. The others winced when the details were revealed.

Carl pointed out possible campsites Raul's men were likely to use. He drew arrows on the map indicating avenues of approach and escape. He described the distances between them and the expected time it would take for them to cover it considering the means by which he expected them to travel.

"There's no rule on killin' on this one. Don't take any chances at all. What we can't reasonably take we'll destroy. We'll need to double the guard, and everyone carries a rifle along with their gun belt." He looked them over again. They all appeared to understand. "If you have any questions or concerns, now's the time to bring them up."

Slate eyed the indications of campsites. "Smitty knows this country like the back of his hand. I wonder if he might have some ideas for contingency plans."

Carl nodded. "Alright. I figured on him as well. We'll confer with him and a few others as this thing unfolds." He rolled the maps up and put them aside. "I'll have a talk with the rest of the boys tomorrow. But no one leaves the ranch after that. No one."

The next morning, Deke and Bobby were mucking out horse stalls and the corral. Their moods were sullen given the labor they were tasked with.

"Well, well, well..." Smitty's crackly voice called out. "Looks like they finally found somethin' suitable for you boys' brains and talents!"

Deke leaned on his shovel and gave the older man a dirty look. Bobby did the same.

"Make sure ya git that one right there." Smitty said, pointing to a horse who had just raised its tail and began defecating. The products of its efforts hitting the ground with a series of wettish 'plops'.

The old man laughed at their plight as he turned to walk away. After he'd taken two steps, warm, wet horse apples splattered against the back of his head, knocking his hat off. He stopped in place and slowly turned around only to see a shirt tail disappear around the corner of the shed. "I'll get 'em for that one!" He mumbled as he scraped the muck from the back of his neck.

Heck and Cotton circled the shed. They saw the prank and had to hold their laughter. They weren't interested in pranks however. They came face to face with the two miscreants.

"Deke, get your gear together. Bobby, you too. We're goin' for a little ride."

The two exchanged glances and dropped their tools where they stood. They explained the situation as they walked. Cotton and Deke were to go to the north road, Heck and Bobby were to go to the south.

The two younger ones were saddled up in a hurry. Three days scant rations were in their saddlebags with lots of ammunition.

Deke slid a new Winchester rifle into his saddle scabbard, compliments of the ranch armory. Bobby did the same.

They rode out together but split up at the fork in the road several miles out. "Ya'll watch yourselves!" Cotton called out.

"Ya'll do the same. See ya in a few days!"

Carl stood on the big stump in the middle of the yard in front of the mess tent. He explained the situation leaving out only certain details he felt were best kept to himself and the others who were at the previous night's meeting. There is such a thing as too much information.

"None of this is to be taken lightly, and don't take no unnecessary chances. Be on guard at all times. I know this a lot different than most of you boys ever done. It's different than anything we've done in the past. Soon as we get word back from Cotton and Heck, we'll go to work."

He swept his gaze across the faces before him. "Any questions?" There were none. Carl picked up one of the heavy leather pouches. He opened it and passed each man one of the large gold coins contained within it.

"This could be the start of a new direction, or it could be a really bad ending for all of us." He warned. "But it's something we're gonna do and we're gonna do it right. There'll be no drinkin' from here on out, and no one leaves the ranch unless I tell them to. Get busy and be ready."

The men broke away and returned to their duties. Most walked away admiring the coin they received. Pedro walked with Raymond and shook his head. "I don't like this, Raymon'. It's a big fight for us."

Raymond agreed. "It'll be a doozy if it don't work out right, that's for sure. But just look at this!" He said holding the coin up in the sunlight.

Smitty spat in the dirt and grumbled to himself. "No drinkin'? Well, damn!"

Carl called Smitty over. The old man spit again figuring his complaint was overheard. "Smitty, saddle up.

You and me's gonna take a ride and look over a few places I been thinkin' about."

Smitty crooked his neck and eyed the man before him. "You got ideas about where to best hit those Molina boys?"

"Yup."

"And you want old Smitty to have a look see?"

"That's right."

"Awright, 'bout time this outfit took notice of my expertise." the old man stated slyly.

Carl folded his arms without expression. "Saddle your horse." He ordered.

Cotton Joe explained the situation to Deke as they rode. He told of the Molina feud and the purpose of their plans. "We don't want to get in their war, but we want to take their stuff, and if that helps out the other side then so be it." He said.

Deke listened to every word. He didn't care either way. He knew Cotton was one who wouldn't say or do anything that didn't have a reason or purpose.

Deke didn't reply. His eyes swept the horizon for signs that would indicate someone was approaching. He saw nothing but blue sky and the far-off hills.

"You'll want to keep them guns clean and loaded." Cotton added.

CHAPTER ELEVEN

Raul Molina stood at the great oaken doors of the Molina Rancho Hacienda. He wore a large sombrero and a yellow silk scarf around his neck. A long, graceful, waxed mustache protruded from his upper lip, twirled at the ends. His posture was erect and rigid, though he sported a pot belly of moderate size. Conchos of various sizes and materials adorned his vest and trouser legs.

He beamed with pride as his men lined up before him in rows two deep and twenty wide, ten on each side. They sat magnificent horses with ornate saddles. They were the best stock bred from the sires and dams of the old country.

The men were loyal to him to the death and he knew it. He expected it and demanded it. They carried a banner with his crest on it. His wife stood at his side, as was her duty to do so. A long black veil shrouded her appearance and downcast countenance, hiding the bruise on her cheek and her cut lip.

The night before, she had attempted to talk to her husband about ending the fight without more bloodshed. It was a mistake born of good intentions. She forgot that good intentions are for the weak. Her husband reminded her of the fact and of her place.

Four wagons, carrying weapons and supplies enough for twice what the men and journey required, were covered with brilliant white canvas. Large yellow caps covered the hubs of the wheels. The teams were outfitted with brilliantly emblazoned harnesses and tack.

In addition to the wagons, a brightly-polished cannon, a four pounder of French origin, accompanied the march. It was a symbol of Raul's power and prestige. He sent it along with an ornate caisson carrying enough shot and powder to feed it for an extended engagement.

All the men wore yellow sashes about their middles, except their leader, who wore one that crossed his chest as well. Armando Agulier saluted with his saber. Raul returned the salute and stepped forward to shake his hand.

"Kill Miguel and Juan. Kill as many of his men as you can. Bring our property back here. You should have no problems, my friend. When you return, we will have a great fiesta!"

Armando sheathed his blade, swelling up at the honor Raul placed on him. "I will do this for you, El

Patron, and the honor of the true Molina Rancho master!" With that, he raised in his stirrups and lifted his arm high. "Vamonos!" He called. A single drum beat rose from the right flank of the formation. The men turned their mounts as Armando galloped to the front of the column. They stepped off in grand fashion.

Raul grinned as they passed, waving to them.

He turned to his wife and lifted her veil. He smiled sweetly at her though she pulled her head back. "My dear, this will all soon be over." She grimaced when he kissed her. Partially out of the twinge of pain it brought and partially from her distaste of the action.

Cotton and Deke were camped at the main point of the south road. They used no fire, eating their rations cold. They never slept at the same time, keeping one man awake and on watch.

The evening of the second day, Deke saw what appeared to be a column of dust rising from the west at a great distance. He went to where Cotton was sleeping and woke him up. Cotton rose rapidly, as if he were wide awake the entire time.

"I think you oughta look at this." Deke said.

The two went back to their lookout point and squirmed into position, both extending long spy glasses. "Yep, I'll bet it's them." Cotton affirmed.

"Want me to go tell the others?" Deke volunteered.

"No, not yet. Let's get a better look at 'em and see what they got. They're still a ways off. It'll take some time for them to get here and they might camp before then. If they do, we'll ease on over for a closer look."

Deke watched the dust intently. He was growing anxious. "It sure looks like a passel of 'em! I wonder what Heck and Bobby are seeing?"

Cotton shook his head. "Probably nothin' judgin' by the size of this bunch." Cotton reached down and started taking his spurs off. Deke followed suit. "If we're gonna be sneakin' around out there, we need to be real quiet." Cotton explained.

Armando led his company long into the day. He sent two men out ahead as lead riders. He sat tall and straight in his saddle. He had earned his position and was proud of it.

He considered his choice of routes. He knew the south road to Mescolare was not a good one, but it would bring him there a half day sooner. It would suffice. He amused himself with thoughts of vanquishing the upstart nephews and returning to the Rancho a hero, carrying their heads in a sack.

Tonight, they would camp. The women would cook good food and they would relax beneath the stars. Some of the vaqueros would play their guitars and sing. He thought of not having his tent put up, but then thought again of the women and entertained the idea of taking one to warm his blankets.

To the south of the road a stream meandered, near in some places and far in others as it turned and twisted in its path. Willows clung to its side and game animals drank and fed from it.

The sun was easing its way below the horizon when Armando turned off the road and gave the command to set up camp.

The company set to work quickly and efficiently. The horses were tethered to long corral ropes picketed in two long lines. They were tended with brushes and combs by their riders and fed with the finest feed from the wagon designated to carry the supplies for the needs of the animals.

Two wagons were positioned in one corner of the camp near the stream, where a large cooking fire was being prepared. The other two were left next to the road, near where the horses were picketed, in order to expedite movement in the morning. The cannon rested in its cradle between the two.

Armando called over a vaquero he considered his sergeant for the purpose of delegating authority among the men. "See to it the guards are posted and the perimeter is secured. Make sure my tent is set up near the stream. The men will eat first. I will have my food in my tent. See to it, that one there, in the blue skirt, brings it to me." He indicated a slender woman who worked beside the others at the supply wagons, preparing food.

The man nodded and saluted, stepping off sharply. He began barking commands before he was three paces away.

The camp was set up in rapid fashion. The smell of food being prepared soon drifted from the supply wagons and spread throughout the camp.

Armando tended his own horse, a great white Andalusian of pure blood lines. It was an animal fit for a man of high office and breeding. It was more precious to him than any other gift of honor bestowed upon him. He brushed it and spoke to it in a soft, low voice. The animal stood still, absorbing the attention. It was as aloof and proud as its master. It remained picketed on a long lead rope near his tent, receiving its own feed from Armando's personal supplies.

Two men, fifty or so yards away; laying low behind a small vegetation covered hill, spied on the camp.

"They got a cannon!" Deke exclaimed in a whisper.

Cotton nodded. "Yup. Didn't know about that one. Guess we'll have to figure a way to get around that." He held his glass to his eye counting the number of men as well as women. His mouth moved as he did so. "Looks like forty men and about... seven women. Fifty horses, countin' the spares, and a couple mules. There's that slick fella in the big tent, he must be the honcho."

The smell of the cooking food reached them. "Damn, that smells good." Deke whispered. His stomach growling.

Cotton nudged him. "I was thinking that too. I've been studying it. There ain't no way to get that far inside and swipe some of that grub." He said, disappointment in his voice.

Deke pulled a cold biscuit from his pocket. "You want half?"

Cotton shook his head. "Nope."

Raul's men sat in close circles. They ate with their legs crossed. Their rifles were stacked in neat pyramids, lined up in rows, muzzles tipped against one another. They spaced their bed rolls out in the same manner in which they rode. The camp was a model of military efficiency, even though they were civilians; They were Raul Molina's personal private army.

Rosaria placed a white cotton cloth over her arm, took up a plate, a bottle of wine, a crystal glass and carried them to Armando's tent. She stopped outside and brushed her long black hair with her fingers, pushing it into place, released the top two buttons of her blouse, smoothed her skirt and spoke. "Señor, your dinner..."

The tent flap opened, Armando waved her in smiling. "Welcome, Señora." He said taking his place at a small table. She placed the plate in front of him and filled the glass with the wine, leaning over just enough to draw his eyes to her bosom.

"Please, join me." He invited. She smiled and sat gracefully in the chair across from him. She had very fine features with an olive complexion. Her hair was dark and soft. The blouse she wore was low on the shoulders, accentuating her long elegant neck line. She had dabbed a hint of perfume on her neck before leaving the supply wagon. She studied him closely while he ate. He was a handsome man, she thought, arrogant and vain, but handsome. She looked around his tent while his attention was averted. He lived lavishly, far above any others she knew. Farther above others, she thought, than he should. She noticed his maps, lying scattered near his bed.

She refilled his glass for the third time, He held the glass up. "Next time bring one for yourself."

She nodded courteously. "I will, if you wish it."

"I wish it." He said. She felt his eyes upon her. "Come over here." She knew what was coming and accepted it. She played coy, just enough to keep him interested. He kissed her, and she surrendered herself to him. "You will bring my dinner every night, Rosaria." He said.

She nodded and smiled again. She cupped his face in her hands, kissing him. "I hope so, Señor."

The night was several hours old. A partial moon rose above the east horizon. The camp lay quiet save for the sounds of snoring and the occasional horse stomping or blowing.

Cotton pointed out the guards, one on each corner of the camp. The one to their right appeared to be fighting off sleep. His head bobbed up and down as he tried to fight the fog of fatigue overcoming him. He soon lost the battle. The one on the left was already snoozing. No one stirred. The horses were tied next to the road, two of the wagons, with the cannon in between, were parked there as well.

Cotton guessed the first one held weapons and ammunition; the other, blankets, tents and other supplies. "We need to sneak up there and get a good look in those wagons." Cotton said. He reached into the road and picked up a handful of horse droppings.

"What are you doing?" Deke questioned.

Cotton handed him another handful and began spreading it on his face and hair!

Deke looked at him as if he'd lost his mind. "I ain't smearin' no horse shit all over me!" He hissed.

"It's a trick an old Indian taught me." Cotton offered. "It'll cover your smell, so the horses won't alert. They'll just think you're another pile of shit." He said with a wink.

Deke rolled his eyes and smeared the manure on himself. "You'd better be right about this."

They scurried across the road, bent low and with no sound, coming to rest next to the first wagon. "You look in here, I'll look in the other one. Don't make any sounds and be careful where you put your hands and feet!" Cotton ordered, then slipped away to the next wagon.

Deke eased around the back of the wagon and peered inside. It was dark, but he could see well enough to make out what was inside. A large canvas tarp covered the contents. He reached inside, but the covering was too far to get a good hold on. He lifted himself up on the tailgate and stepped gingerly inside, then carefully pulled the canvas back, revealing stacks of rifles and boxes of ammunition. There were a few kegs of powder as well.

There was a large lump in the middle of the canvas, so he pulled it back farther.

His eyes went wide when he recognized the form of a Gatling gun. He swallowed hard and went to replace the cover when he saw a long wooden rod lying next to the weapon. It appeared to be a cleaning rod kept with the gun. An idea flashed in his mind. He snatched it up and stuck it halfway in one of the barrels. He pulled out his knife and scored deeply around it then snapped it off. He used the other end to shove it down into the barrel. He replaced the cover and cautiously looked around before slipping out of the wagon and returning to the side where he started.

Looking over, he saw Cotton kneeling next to the cannon. He couldn't make out what he was doing, other than fidgeting with the left wheel axle hub. He saw him jerk and nearly fall. Cotton caught himself, looked around and motioned Deke to move back across the road.

They took their original places and turned to see if anyone moved. Nothing. There was stillness in the camp. Deke's heart beat in his ears.

"What's that?" Cotton asked pointing at Deke's hand. Deke looked down and realized he'd carried the broken cleaning rod with him. He quickly told him what he had done.

Cotton held up a large, bent cotter pin. "That cannon ain't gonna go too far tomorrow. Dang near couldn't get it out. It'll slow 'em down a might. They ain't gonna leave that behind!"

The two snaked their way back from their positions and moved back to their earlier camp. They gathered up their gear and got set to ride hard back to the ranch. "You go get Heck and Bobby. I'll meet ya'll back at the home place!"

They rode through the night. Deke came up on Heck and Bobby late the following morning. He couldn't know exactly where they were, so he trotted down the road, thinking they'd see him.

A rock bounced off the ground in front of him. He looked up the hill and saw Bobby waving at him. Bobby pointed to a trail that would lead him up to where they were.

"Deke's coming up." He hollered over at Heck. Heck walked into the clearing, looking around.

Deke rode in just as he saw him. "Me and Cotton got a good look at 'em. They're on the south road travelin' like some kind of circus. They got enough hardware for a war. They even got a cannon!"

Heck and Bobby exchanged glances. "Better get back and get this thing goin'."

They quickly gathered up the meager gear they had around and tightened the cinches on their mounts. "Let's get on back and get set up." Heck said.

They rode fast, too fast for any talking. Deke's horse was just about played out, but Deke urged him on. He still carried the broken off Gatling cleaning rod.

Tracy T. Thurman

CHAPTER TWELVE

When they finally made it back to the ranch, they discovered that Cotton had already been there long enough to tell what they had seen.

"You reckon we oughta send a rider down to Miguel and let him know?"

Carl shook his head and smirked. "Hell, they probably knew yesterday."

There was a lot of activity. Slate and Smitty were saddled up, getting ready to take up position where they figured the Raul Molina company would camp the next night. They would do their jobs and meet up with Carl and the rest afterward.

They were to try and poison Raul's water barrels with a concoction Flap Jacks made up. It was carried in two brown bottles, one by each man. It wouldn't outright kill them, but by the time their stomach and bowels settled they'd probably wish they were dead.

It'd slow them down for a good day. It was a risky plan considering where in the camp the wagons containing the water barrels were placed. Unless of course they placed them differently because of the terrain where they stopped.

That concoction also had the effect of making a few fellas even more nervous about the possibility of getting on the bad side of the old buffalo soldier turned outlaw cook.

Smitty had an idea about sabotaging the cannon. He made a ball of gunpowder, kerosene and wax. His plan was to ram it into the gun with some more powder behind it. It wouldn't be a lot, but it would be enough to blow Raul Molina's symbol of power and prestige into a lot of hot, man-killing pieces, destroying the weapon.

Smitty's eyes lit up like a kid on Christmas when he explained his plan. "That thang'll go to smithereens! It'll make a hell of a noise!"

Slate had warned him to not get carried away. "You don't want to get caught by them boys, old man. They'll skin your scrawny carcass and make ya wear your own ass like a hat!"

Smitty stuck his chin out. "Who you callin' scrawny?"

Deke learned that Bill, Pedro and Raymond had left to cause a rock slide on the road about twenty miles from the Molina's present position, where there was already an unstable overhang of rocks and boulders. It would look like a natural event and shouldn't raise any suspicions. Afterward, they were to move east and south as the road curved about the same distance, perhaps where the column might stop again, and wait for the others.

He figured Bill must have raised hell about that assignment. But Bill wasn't one you'd send on a job that required stealth.

Carl walked toward Deke as he was stripping the gear from his horse. The horse was lathered up and tired. It trotted away and rolled in the dust, then sat there for minute before getting back up and shaking off.

Deke scooped some grain and forked some hay over for the animal. He knew it had earned a good rest. He leaned on the railing for a minute or two watching the bay shake off the dust and sweat. The animal moseyed to the feed bin and ate heartily. He liked that horse. They'd already been through a lot together.

"I hear you and Cotton make a pretty good team." Carl said.

"We just did what we were told. Them fella's ain't expecting much trouble yet."

Carl nodded. "You're right. Cotton told me about the cannon and Gatling gun. That was a big risk you took. But a good idea. I hope we get to see them fire that thing."

Deke smiled big. Carl was visually proud of him. "You're makin' a good hand, Deke." Carl said, before he walked away. Higher praise no man had ever heard. Deke felt a foot taller and proud. He'd never felt that way before.

Deke went to get cleaned up, but stopped by the mess tent first, hoping to find something hot to eat. He saw Cotton at the table, his cheeks bulging as he chewed. The smell of that Mexican grub was still on his mind and still causing his stomach to grumble.

"I hope that ain't got none of Flap Jacks' poison mixed in it." He said as he sat down."

"I heard dat boy!" Flap Jacks called. The man appeared with his hands on his hips and a towel thrown over his shoulder. "You gonna eat or not?"

Deke's face turned red. "Yes, sir." He said.

"Well git you a plate. Or you just feel like talkin?" Flap Jacks looked at both of them sideways. "You boys been rollin in a manure pile?"

"Why ya ask that?" Cotton replied, knowing full well the reason.

"Cause, you boys got hoss crap all over you!"

Deke spoke up. "It's an old Indian trick, keeps from spookin' the horses. They think you're just another pile of shit."

Flap Jacks' eyes widened, and he leaned his back. "Whatever you say boy, whatever you say..."

Deke got up, grabbed a plate and a big spoon. He loaded up on beef and beans, grabbed a couple hot biscuits and started in across from Cotton who was just finishing up. Deke had his mouth full when Cotton suddenly doubled over holding his stomach and groaning.

Deke dropped his spoon like it suddenly grew thorns, desperately spitting his food out.

Cotton straightened up, pointed at him and started laughing. Flap Jacks did the same from behind him. "Now you gonna clean dat mess up!"

Deke grumbled, picked up his spoon and started eating again, slowly. He finished his meal and took his plate to the wash basin. A long slender arm took it from him. "I'll get it Deke. You better go and clean up." He looked over and saw Doralee smiling at him as if he were a child.

"Don't you go getting dat boy spoiled now!" Came Flap Jacks' voice.

Deke nodded thanks and hurried on his way.

******

Bill leaned into the pry bar while Raymond pushed with his feet. Pedro dug under the boulder. The dust to the west had stopped moving, allowing them more time to get the job done. Bill cursed viciously at the rock that represented the lowly task to which he was assigned.

They worked hard, all while trying to keep an eye out for advanced riders. Finally, the big rock budged. Bill grabbed up the bar and found a purchase spot to place it. He heaved on it while the other two dug and pushed. It budged some more. Bill re-positioned the bar again. Their shirts were soaked with sweat and dirt. Pedro's knuckles bled as did Raymond's.

"Here she goes!" Bill exclaimed.

The boulder tumbled with a great roar bringing down much of the hillside with it! Pedro nearly lost his footing. Raymond grabbed him and pulled him up.

"Gracias amigo!" Pedro exclaimed.

Dirt and debris fell from above, pouring over the road. A dust cloud rose, covering them and filling their eyes and nostrils. The men choked and moved quickly away.

Bill stood back and watched the cloud rise into the air. "They're likely to see that!"

"We'd better get on outta here then." Raymond suggested.

Pedro nodded insistently. "Si. We better go!"

They quickly made ready and spurred their mounts eastward to where they were to meet Carl and the others.

******

Rosaria stepped from the tent before the sun was up, buttoning her blouse and smoothing her clothes. Only the guards were awake. They eyed the form of the woman as she made her departure, exchanging lewd expressions. She knew they were watching and didn't care. They were nothings and would remain nothings.

When she made her way back to the wagons, she stepped into the stream and washed. She was not a self-conscious woman, but she made sure she was covered by the bushes that lined the banks of the water. She was quick and dressed again before anyone noticed.

The camp stirred. Men rolled up their blankets in their ground sheets and tied them in neat bundles. The fire was stoked, and coals spread out to facilitate cooking.

The women were working on the morning meal. Large frying pans were filled with sizzling bacon; two-gallon coffee pots brewed next to the coals. They had made tortillas the night before and were now warming them on a large metal sheet. They cooked, cleaned and labored at the wagons and fire while the men prepared the camp to move.

Armando stepped from his tent and stretched. He was smiling brightly, tucking in his shirt. He wrapped his sash about him and adjusted it carefully in place. His boots sported heavy spurs, were elaborately etched, and had large silver rowels. He pulled them on and stood. He called to his sergeant. "We will move in one hour. No less!" The man nodded, saluted and moved about the men ordering them to hurry up.

Breakfast was ready, but no food could be served until the stock was cared for, saddled, harnessed up and ready to travel. Armando's tent and trappings were broken down, folded and carefully stowed away.

He walked among the men as they performed their tasks. He carried with him a riding crop he used to point out things that needing adjusting or redone to suit his liking. When all was accomplished the men descended on the wagons and hurried through a line getting their plates filled. They sat in circles as they had the night before and ate in silence.

Rosaria brought a plate to Armando who sat under a tree on a blanket. "Your breakfast, Señor." She smiled deeply and forced herself to blush. He returned her smile and accepted the plate.

"Please, sit with me and enjoy this beautiful morning." She did as requested. He ate his food slowly and with the air of a gentleman. She giggled and handed him a napkin. She filled a glass with water and handed that as well. He breathed deeply when he was done. He withdrew a pouch from his pocket, tobacco and papers contained inside.

"Allow me..." She offered. He tilted his head and handed her the pouch. She deftly rolled a cigarette. Her hands were small with long graceful fingers. Licking the paper edge and sealing it, she placed it in his lips and lit a match. He leaned forward, drawing in the smoke, then exhaling as he returned to his reclined position. His eyes never left her.

"What do you think we will do today?" She asked.

He waved a hand in the air. "We will travel another day, and camp tonight. We have time to make it to Mescolare and to deal with Miguel and his gang of cut-throats if they want to make a fight"

"I fear for your safety, Señor." She said.

He looked at her surprised. "Why do you do that?"

"I mean, there could be a big fight and you could get hurt."

"Do not fear for me, Senorita. This is child's play. I will easily win any battle Miguel wishes to bring. I am superior in every way."

He swept his arm about the camp as the men hustled to finish their work. "I have an army and weapons, the best horses in the country; I am smarter and faster, and besides, all I have to do is meet a wagon and bring it back to the Rancho…"

She laid her head on his shoulder. "If you say so. Señor, if you say so."

He stood from his place then. "We must go. I will see you tonight." He took her hand and kissed it gallantly.

Rosaria took her leave and returned to her wagon. The other women gave her looks of jealousy in some and contempt in others. Maria, the mother figure of them all, especially disliked her. Rosaria barely noticed as her mind was busy with other things; other things, miles down the road.

They traveled in the same manner as the day before. A rider came to the front of the column. "Señor. We must stop for a while. The cannon has broken!"

Armando held his arm up. "What do you mean, the cannon has broken?" He snapped.

"Come see. It has fallen off its wheel."

Armando wheeled his horse around and galloped to the wagons. The cannon sat crooked in the road. The left wheel had indeed come off. A long drag mark extended behind it.

"How did this happen?" The men who bore responsibility for the weapon were scurrying about retrieving the wheel and inspecting the damage to the axle.

"I don't know, Señor. It was fine when we left the Rancho." He shrugged.

Armando stepped from his saddle and looked at it closely. The threads that held the large nut in place were worn from being dragged on the road. A man rolled the wheel up while the others dug through the rear wagon for the wagon jack.

Armando slapped his riding crop against his leg. Damaging the cannon was something that would bring the ire of Raul. It was one of the jewels of his ascendancy.

"Can you fix it?" Armando asked.

"Si. We can fix it. But it will take some time. Not long, but some time."

Armando stepped back into his stirrups. "Very well. We will go ahead, I will leave a guard detail with you. You will fix Señor Molina's cannon and catch up with us when you are finished. Make sure there are no marks on it!"

He rode back to the front of the column. He didn't want to take the cannon along in the first place, but Raul insisted on it for only one purpose; he wanted it seen. Armando designated four men to stay with the cannon and its crew until it was repaired. They rode back to where the weapon stood leaning awkwardly on its left axle.

He raised his arm again and the column continued forward.

******

Slate saw the dust rise up in the air from where the rockslide should be. A moment later he heard the rumble of the debris falling from the hill.

"Boy, that'll sure make a mess!" He exclaimed. The others nodded. They were nearly where they wanted to be, scanning for a good place to hide out and wait where they could get a good look at what was coming. The dust to the west had begun to rise again, telling them the column was on the move.

They settled in behind a hill and squirmed to the top where they could look down on the road. Two riders approached wearing yellow sashes. Slate, his rifle in hand, watched as they passed. He calculated the distance to be no more than about sixty yards. He could put them both down with two easy shots. It wasn't time for that sort of thing, however. They settled in to wait and watch the road.

The two riders saw the dust and heard the rumble about the same time Heck and the others did. They kicked their horses into a gallop. The rock slide was complete, effectively blocking the road. A horse and rider could get around it but there was no way to get a wagon past. It would have to be cleared and that was going to be a difficult task. They turned and rode back to the column.

Smitty eyed the area south of the road. It was wide open, with tall grass that might help conceal a man if he was careful. It was narrow with a rise on the far side of it. It was a perfect campsite, a mile or so from the slide. He expected they'd have to stop there.

"You see how that slope moves up there on the south?" Smitty indicated. "They ain't gonna park no wagons on uneven ground." He pointed his finger left and right across the area. "They'll be spread out some. They'll send men to try and clear that slide. They'll be a good distance away. That'll sure cut down on the ones in the camp. If everything goes right, we oughta be able to slip in and slip back out. They still ain't expectin' no trouble and they'll have their minds on other thangs."

Slate looked and listened as Smitty laid out the idea. He nodded and confirmed the old man's insights. He looked over at him and slapped him on the back. "You still ain't worth a damn as a cattleman."

Smitty grinned in response. "You got that right."

The riders loped back to the column and reined up in front their leader. They told of the rockslide up ahead. "It will take a long time to clear it." one of them reported.

Armando looked up at the sky and cursed. "Why this bad luck?" He rode on in silence for a while pondering his next move, then shook his head. "Take some men, move ahead and start to work. We will be there this afternoon."

"There is a place to camp only a mile or so from it. If you wish to wait there until the work is done."

"I will consider it. Now go."

The men rode back to the rear wagon selecting five men to accompany them. They drew shovels and tools and galloped their mounts back ahead of the column.

Armando looked behind him as the column closed up in the spaces vacated by those who rode ahead. His mind was working. The cannon was far behind him now, a rockslide blocking their path ahead. This seemed to be too much of a coincidence. His eyes narrowed, and he searched the area around him. He considered the situation and rode on.

******

Cotton, Deke and Bobby sat around the table in the house. Carl had his maps laid out with marks indicating the travel of the Molina column.

"If Slate and the boys are able to pull off their job, them fella's oughta be good and sick about halfway through the next day. They ain't gonna be up to much of a fight or even a chase."

Deke leaned forward on his elbows. His eyes were wide, absorbing the maps and the strategical thinking Carl was demonstrating.

"I figure this is where we'll raise hell with 'em." Carl said, pointing at a place that was backed up by a mountain to the south and showed several pencil drawn trails leading out to the north.

"Bill, Pedro, and Raymond are gonna meet us there. We'll wait till it's nice and dark. Bill and his boys will start shooting up the wagons about midnight. We'll slide in and swipe them horses." He pointed at Cotton, "Watch for the guards. Have your sights fixed on 'em. If they stay in place after the others start the ball rollin', put 'em down." Cotton nodded in the affirmative.

******

Juan stood on the roof of the cantina, a spyglass extended to the south. "They're coming, brother!" He slapped the glass closed and climbed down the ladder. Miguel smiled brilliantly, turning to address his men, which had grown in number to thirty. "Raul has sent forty men, horses, weapons and supplies to intercept our silver!" He announced. "Our gringo friends have slowed them down, but they won't stop them. Today we take what is ours and begin to regain our Rancho!"

The men cheered. "Viva La Molina! Death to the Raul's!"

Juan climbed into his saddle next to his brother. "Let's go get our silver, brother." They rode out toward the approaching troop of Mexican soldiers, rifles at the ready. Miguel drew the gleaming sword of his ancestors.

Capitan Enrique Martinez saw the approaching riders. He looked back at the wagon and fifteen tired guards flanking it. They had been riding for weeks, bringing the wagon from deep in Mexico. He halted the column, turned to face them and withdrew a folded paper from his vest, opened it up, and began reading. He then held the paper above his head for the others to see. "I have orders to stop here." He said. He then pointed to the men riding behind. "You men are to return to the fort. You must ride fast. Now go. All of you! Go!" The men looked at each other with questioning glances, milling around in uncertainty. The men guarding the wagon and the driver did the same. Enrique folded the paper and replaced it in his pocket, repeated his order and withdrew his pistol. "Go, I say. GO! Do not turn back or I will shoot you myself!" The men turned their mounts and galloped off leaving a trail of dust behind them.

"Señor? What are we to do?" asked one of the guards.

He looked them over one by one. You will obey my orders, Corporal, or you will die." He said plainly.

He turned his mount to take position behind the wagon and ordered them to move out. They traveled in silence, save for the occasional squeak of the wagon wheels.

Miguel's men drew nearer. When they were close, they kicked their mounts into a gallop and quickly encircled the wagon. The guards raised their hands looking about in fear.

Miguel rode directly to their Capitan and pointed his pistol at his head. He cursed him loudly and drew the hammer back. The Corporal who had spoken earlier, seeing his leader in trouble, took the chance of grabbing his weapon. He fell in a fusillade of gunfire, toppling like a shapeless sack from his saddle, he was dead before he hit the ground.

"You see!" Miguel called out to them. "You see! It is useless! Do not die for no reason! I will take this wagon for myself and your Capitan as my hostage! You men go back! Go back and tell them the rightful heir, Miguel Molina; the rising son of the Molina Rancho has taken what is his! If I am followed, I will kill this man! I will tear him apart between my horses and scatter his parts in the desert! Now, GO!"

The driver of the wagon leaped from the seat and climbed aboard the dead man's horse. He and the three remaining soldiers needed no further incentive. They yanked their mounts about and ran into the distance as if their shirt-tails were on fire.

Juan slid from his saddle and yanked the dusty tarp off the wagon. Old crates were stacked side by side and end to end. The writings on the crates was in an old, gracefully flourished script, barely legible. He pried one of them open revealing the silver bars and coins of different shapes inside. He withdrew one of the bars, feeling the weight of it, then passed it to Miguel. He shoved his pistol back in its holster, grinned widely and held the bar up. The others saw the gleam of the sun on it and cheered.

Miguel handed the bar back to his brother. "We will have plenty of time to celebrate Grandfather's legacy, but now we must go. There is a long distance between here and the hacienda."

He motioned to man at his right. "Go forward and verify my boats and mules are in place, then return. Tell the men to be ready."

The man nodded and sped off.

Capitan Enrique Martinez looked at his captors and at Miguel "You are a cruel man, Señor." He said. "Tearing a man apart between horses? That is barbaric!"

Miguel leaned over shoved him. "My friend, it is good to see you! It has been a long time since we were in school together at the Citadel."

"It is good to see you also, my friend, and to know this treasure is with its rightful owner. It has been a long time." He motioned at Juan. "He was just a boy then, two classes behind. He has only gotten uglier!"

Juan turned his head left and right. "You only wish you were as handsome as me!"

The three enjoyed the reunion, but there was still much work to do. They turned west on the fork of the road. A landing lay several miles ahead where there were boats waiting to carry the crates across. A small herd of pack mules waited on the side, held by some of Miguel's men.

"That was a smart thing you did, sending those men back." Miguel mentioned.

Enrique nodded, pulling the folded paper from his vest pocket. "I didn't want them all killed, so I read my orders and sent them away."

"What orders were those?"

"These orders." Enrique said, passing the paper to him.

Miguel unfolded the paper and scanned it. He turned it over and did the same.

"There is nothing written here?"

Enrique smiled. "I know..."

He tossed the paper aside and grinned. "I have some clothes for you to change into. We will bloody your uniform and leave it behind. They will think you've been killed."

Enrique accepted the situation. He could not return and face the military inquisition he knew would be convened, too many questions would be asked, and Raul's influence was very strong there. He would resign himself to being remembered as a murdered hero in his homeland. There was a better life, a wealthier life waiting for him ahead. He looked forward to it with great anticipation.

******

Armando halted the column. He studied the site the rider had told him about. It wasn't the ideal place, but it was the best that was available. He wanted to be ready to move out first thing in the morning, with no delays.

He considered how much time he'd already lost and planned to make it up the following two days going into Mescolare. He knew the shipment he was to receive would be there soon. He could not risk missing it, or his life would become worthless. Raul entrusted him with this mission and failure was unthinkable.

He looked for a messenger to appear from Mescolare, but one hadn't arrived as yet. That could mean one of two things. The shipment was not yet near, or the man had been caught. He knew not to count on it either way.

He ordered the column to remain in line but ease off the road. The south side of the camp gradually rose into the side of a bluff. He figured it to be a fairly well defensible site if the need arose. He gave his orders and called upon his sergeant to see the camp was settled correctly, then spurred on ahead to look at the landslide that had halted them.

The men labored hard shoveling dirt and prying rocks out of the road. Dirt clung to them, adhering to the sweat. Many were bleeding at their arms, hands and knees. One man had a rough bandage around his head covering a wound from a falling rock. The hillside was still unstable and continued to pour down debris.

"How long do you think?" Armando asked one of the men.

The man turned around, breathing heavily, and leaned on his shovel. "It will take most of the night, Señor. We will need more men when you can send them."

He stood in his stirrups and surveyed the pile of rocks and dirt, gritted his teeth and shook his head. "I will send them right away, and I will send canteens and food as well."

"Gracias, Señor." the man replied. "Gracias." He then turned and returned to his work.

When Armando rode back, the camp was already set up, the women were busy preparing food. The wagons were parked just as they were, ready to travel. They had opened a space between the second and third one for the Cannon to be positioned when it returned. Picket ropes were stretched in neat lines just as before. Their horses tied in place, the men were busy caring for their mounts. The sergeant had ordered them to leave their saddles on but to loosen their cinches.

Armando rode to them and pointed out several of their number. "Take canteens, two each, and some food and go forward to help clear our way." He ordered.

The men, quickly and without question, complied.

More men were sent ahead to help with the excavation of the road. His tent was in place and he entered it with a slap of the covering.

Slate and Smitty sprawled on the hill watching the proceedings. "That'll work fine." Smitty whispered. "Just fine."

Slate watched the tall man on the fine white horse with the yellow sash across his chest. "I bet that there'd be the honcho."

"I always wanted to kill me a fancy dude like that." Smitty said.

"We'll lay low 'till well after dark. Them boys'll be mighty tired by then. We'll slip in, and slip out, none the wiser. You just hold your powder. There'll be plenty of time to kill fancy dudes."

******

Armando lay in his tent on the bed of blankets and pillows. His brow was furrowed as he studied the top of the canvas. His boots lay by the door where he had removed them.

"Your dinner, Señor." Came the soft feminine voice of Rosaria.

"Come in." He said.

She entered carrying a plate, wine and two glasses. He sat up and moved to his table. She placed the food before him as before, leaning closer to him as she did. The scent of her perfume intoxicated him, carrying away his present worries, if only for the moment. She sat across from him and poured his glass, then, not waiting to be invited, poured her own. She watched him eat and drink from his glass.

"You are troubled, Señor…" She spoke softly.

He nodded, gulping another drink of wine. "Yes, it has been a difficult day."

There was a sound just outside the entrance to his tent. "Señor!"

"What is it?!" He asked sharply.

"Señor. The cannon has returned and is in place." came the answer.

"Fine! That is good! Be off with you!"

The sound of retreating footsteps faded.

"We have lost a lot of time. We must go at first light." He shook his head and emptied his glass.

She refilled it, still smiling. She held her glass up. He did the same. "Salute, Señor." He nodded and smiled. "Salute, Señora."

She moved his plate away, unbuttoned her blouse and stepped to his bed. Armando tossed his napkin over his shoulder and joined her.

******

Again, the fragrance of the campfire and food teased the men hiding in the cover of the bushes and rocks. Smitty unconsciously smacked his lips.

"Stop that!" Slate ordered.

"Stop what?"

"Smackin' your damn jaws!"

Smitty swallowed hard and clamped his teeth together.

Presently they heard the hoofbeats and wheels on the road. The cannon moved into its position, none the worse for wear. However, the men accompanying it were clearly very fatigued. They dragged themselves into the camp and dropped in place.

The sergeant moved men to and from the place of the rock slide, allowing some to rest while others took their places. The work continued into the night. There were spells when all was very quiet, then moments when it was very busy during the times when men traded places and gathered more supplies.

A half-moon eased its way over the eastern horizon. It hung there, working its way into the sky. The men in the camp had recently changed shifts. Even the guards were taken to work on removing the blockage.

Slate nudged Smitty indicating the moon. "We'd better get this done if we're going to before that thing lights the place up." Smitty agreed.

They each carried a brown bottle of the concoction Flap Jacks worked up. Smitty carried his 'cannon ball'. Each wagon carried two water barrels. The two cooking wagons also had a flour barrel and other accoutrements. The women were in their own tent near the wagons. Any sound would bring them out and the alarm would sound loudly after that. Everyone it seemed, was fast asleep.

The two outlaws slipped across the road soundlessly. Slate at the front two wagons, Smitty at the back two. They quickly lifted barrel lids and peered inside. Spilling a dollop of the brown bottle in each. He eased around the opposite side of the wagons and treated those barrels as well. His job complete, Slate snuck around to the road side of the wagon and looked for Smitty. He couldn't be seen. He looked and moved the direction of where he should be.

He saw him then, crouched down in the tall grass under the wagon. Someone was rustling around at the rear of the wagon. Slate ducked back, looking under the wagon past Smitty. He could see two legs and the bottom part of a woman's skirt. They were whispering. A woman giggled. He craned his neck as they quietly walked away into the far shadows carrying a bottle of wine.

Smitty looked over at Slate and shrugged his shoulders. Slate motioned for him to hurry up. One thing for sure, Slate noticed, was the old man could sure move quietly. He glided across the grass like a snake. Once finished he slipped back, reached in his coat and took out the 'cannon ball' he'd manufactured. They watched carefully, then Smitty motioned for Slate to grab the ram rod attached to the side of the carriage. He slipped a cloth bag of powder and the ball into the bore of the weapon. Grabbing the rod, he shoved it deep into the barrel and seated it. Then he replaced the rod.

The sound of approaching men and horses came from the direction of the rock slide. With a quick look, the two men scurried back across the road to their earlier positions. They had no more than ducked into the bushes when a group of men appeared on the road where they had been.

Two men carrying an arm load of canteens swung down and began filling them at the water barrels. Two other men ambled into the camp and found their bedrolls while two more emerged and took their horses.

Slate and Smitty squirmed away and worked themselves back to their horses and led them, walking, far back along the trail they had come in on earlier. They walked until daylight then swung into saddle and rode to catch up with Carl and the others.

******

Miguel halted his men next to the boats. There were four of them, flat bottomed and wide, lined up on the bank of the river; small skiffs that would hold only a moderate amount of weight. There were ropes tied to either end of them, so they could be pulled back and forth. They would move the crates to the mules then swim their horses across after destroying the wagon and placing Enrique's blood stained uniform next to it.

The mules were tethered on the other side. The men holding them watched the approach and waved. The river was narrower here and, as the spring rains were long since past. It wasn't running very deep or fast.

Juan swam his mount to the other side along with ten of the men. Miguel remained at the wagon and directed the loading of the crates. Juan's horse pawed up the embankment and shook the water off. Juan stepped from the saddle and greeted the men holding the mules. "Are you ready for a long, hard journey?"

They nodded in return, "Si..."

Juan looked them over then halted. "There is supposed to be six of you. I see only five. Where is the other man?"

The men looked at each other and held their heads down. "One has left, Señor, last night he left."

Juan was clearly disturbed. "How did five of you not see a man leave, even in the middle of the night?" They shrugged and shuffled their feet.

Juan walked around the area studying it, looking for sign. He walked their camp. In the bushes, next to the river he found what he expected. He reached his arm in and removed a large, empty bottle. There were several of them there. He strode back to the men, infuriated.

He held the bottle up. "You were drunk!" He snarled.

The situation did not bode well for the group of men, not at all.

"Which one of you is in charge here?" Juan asked.

A man stepped forward, a man Juan knew to be one who had a particularly lazy streak. He was a good mule handler that was the only reason he remained with the outfit.

"Tell me Pepe, did you not know the importance of this operation? Did you not know the importance of your job?"

The man's eyes searched the ground his head down, shoulders slumped. "He brought the bottles of tequila from town, Señor. We were very thirsty and tired. I didn't think it would hurt to...."

"You didn't think!" Juan cut him off. "You didn't think! That is your problem, Pepe! You don't THINK!"

The man tried to smile and assume a posture of innocence. Juan sneered at him and brought the empty bottle crashing down on the man's head with tremendous force.

The man crumpled to the ground blood oozing from the wound in his scalp. His skull was cracked from the blow, his head began swelling. The others instinctively moved to help him. Juan yanked his side arm and pointed it at them. "Let him be! He will lie there. I should shoot every one of you!" The men froze in place. He held them there for a long moment, considering the situation.

Juan holstered his weapon. "As it is, we are now two men short. You will have to make up the difference and work that much harder! When Raul's men show up, you will be the first to face them."

Miguel and the others could see the disturbance on the other side of the river. "What is going on there?" one of them asked.

Miguel shrugged. "I don't know but watch closely so your memory will be refreshed about what happens when you anger my brother."

They removed the crates from the wagon and placed them gently in the boats. Then, carefully hauled them across one after another. When a boat was emptied, it was hauled back, and the process repeated. Enrique changed out of his uniform into the clothes Miguel gave him. They were fine clothes, better than any he'd worn since he was a boy. They fit snug in places, but he wore them with confidence, though he felt odd and out of place to not be in his uniform.

When the last boat was emptied, Juan ordered Pepe to be loaded in the boat and sent across. The man groaned and whimpered, his eyes bulged from behind swollen lids. Enrique laid his uniform neatly, and in order against the side of a small rise in the sand. He stepped back, drew his revolver, and shot it full of holes.

They dragged Pepe out of the boat. Miguel took the uniform, tore it in shreds and soaked it with the man's blood. "It's a good thing Juan did this. I thought we would have to kill a horse."

In a short matter of time, the uniform Capitan Enrique Martinez had worn proudly for years was bloody and torn, scattered near the wagon. Miguel placed a hand on his friend's shoulder. "You will be remembered by them as a hero, my friend. We will build you a fine hacienda and find you a beautiful wife. Let this be gone from you and look to your future."

Enrique nodded, he looked at the remains of it, stood in his stirrups and saluted. "It is time to put that behind." He replied.

As the last of the men guided their mounts into the water, the wagon was set ablaze. "What of him?" Enrique asked, pointing at Pepe. Miguel nudged the man with his boot. Rolling him over until he fell into the water, then, without comment, stepped into his stirrups and proceeded to the other side.

******

"Señor! A rider approaches!" Armando stood in his stirrups and looked to where the man pointed. A rider galloped toward them, a red sash streaming from his upheld rifle. He motioned the men at his sides to accompany him and rode to meet the messenger.

The man's horse was played out. When he brought it to a halt, it stood shaking, its knees wobbling. The animal was lathered head to tail, breathing laboriously.

"Miguel has the treasure, Señor! He is loading it on mules and moving to the west along the river."

Armando cursed viciously. "Come to the wagons, get some water and food. We will talk there."

The column was halted, awaiting his orders. The man slipped from his saddle and nearly fell from exhaustion. His horse stumbled away and dropped to its side panting desperately.

"You've ruined your horse." Armando said.

The man drank water thirstily. "Si, Señor. He was a good one. He never stopped. I am sorry for him, but I felt the need to ride as quickly as I could. I thought you would be closer by now."

Armando nodded. He handed the man his pistol. "Put the animal down now. He needs not suffer any longer."

The man took the weapon in a trembling hand, walked to his horse, pointed the gun behind its ear and pulled the trigger. The animal jerked, then lay still. The man lowered his head and returned the weapon to Armando. "He was a good one." He repeated.

"You will have another. Now tell me of Miguel."

The man explained the activities at the river. An advance rider had told them about the wagon and the Army Capitan. He also explained how he coaxed the others into getting drunk, so he could make his escape.

Armando smiled at the man. "You've done well, my friend. You've done well." He spread a map on the tailgate of the wagon, placing a rock on it to hold it in place. "Show me where they are. Do you know this area well?"

The man pointed to the place on the river. Then, he took a pencil and drew a trail that would lead them on an intercept course. "It is not an easy road for wagons, Señor, but it will do."

Armando was very disturbed and angry. But he was pleased with the information the man provided. "We will turn south now." He ordered.

The man stood where he was looking at him as if he were waiting for something. "What is it?" He asked impatiently.

"Señor, the Patron said if I do this I will receive a great reward and be allowed to go."

The statement grated against Armando's already raw nerves. He looked at the man as though his presence was that of something filthy. "You coward. You ask to be paid a ransom then expect to run away?"

The man's face grew pale. "N- No Señor! Only the Patron said…"

Armando struck him, slapping him hard across the face. "You will ride with us and you will serve in the place you are required to! You will fight, and you will do your duty! Then, if it so pleases ME, you will receive your reward."

The man shamefully nodded and stepped backwards. "S-Si, Señor!" The man crept away, stepping to his dead horse and began the struggle of removing his saddle. At Armando's direction, another horse was brought to him. Two others remained with him to see that he made it to the column.

Armando spoke to the men in the lead column telling them they were turning south. "It will be rough traveling, but we must move quickly." Just then a man leaned over and vomited intensely. He then leapt from his mount and hurried into the bushes. Another did the same. Then another…

"What is going on here?!" Armando demanded.

Two women climbed down from the wagons, fell to their hands and knees and got sick on the ground. One of the men from the rear of the column approached. "Señor, the men are ill, all of them. Everybody has become sick!"

Armando grimaced. He felt hot and cold at the same time. He leaped from his saddle and knelt on the ground, holding his stomach, he got sick in the grass.

The column was halted where it stood. The entire camp was incapacitated. "What is this? What is this?!" Armando called out to the sky. "Is this punishment? What have I done to deserve this?"

He stood and walked among the men, horses and wagons. His stomach cramped painfully. Armando's mind was racing blindly through the cloud of sickness that swept over him. He looked about, saw and smelled the results of the illness among his column. The events of the last few days flowed together. Adding them up, he came to startling and infuriating conclusion!

"We have been sabotaged!" He screamed. "Damn you! Damn you!" He screamed into the distance. "Dump the water barrels! Empty your canteens!" He yelled slapping one away from the mouth of a man drinking. The men began to shakily comply. He strode deliberately along the sides of the wagons unlashing the ropes and straps that held the water barrels and toppled them onto the ground! He screamed in rage as moved along. "Damn You! Damn you!"

One of the women, Maria approached him. She looked miserable and quite sad. "Señor, I can make medicine for us and stop this sickness, but I need water." Armando asked her to repeat herself, which she did. "I can make the medicine, Señor..."

"Very well." He pointed at two men who didn't look as bad as the others. "Go to the stream and fill the canteens. As many as you can carry. You must hurry!" The woman briefly said something else. He leaned his head down to hear her, then shouted after the man. "And rinse them out first!" The men nodded and rushed to their horses. The stream was not far away for a healthy man, but for one whose body is purging itself from both ends it could seem like a mighty long way.

The woman busied herself at the tailgate of her wagon. A rock sitting on it was swept away with her hand as she began gathering the necessary ingredients for the medicine. She took roots, powders and herbs, some tree bark and a handful of tea leaves, and began grinding and combining them in a large bowl. She placed more of the ingredients in more bowls and instructed the other women to do the same.

Presently the two riders returned and piled the canteens next to the wagon where the women worked. Armando received the first of the antidote. He gulped it down, needing to clamp his hand tightly over his own mouth in order to force himself to swallow it.

"Are you sure this will work, Señora?" He gasped, shuddering at the lingering taste in his mouth.

"Yes, Señor, I am sure." She smiled apologetically.

They poured the concoction in some buckets and gave each man a cup full as they filed by. It was bitter and thick. The men grimaced as they gulped the medicine. He sent more men to gather canteens and fill them. They would refill their barrels once the wagons reached the water.

Rosaria stepped before him, she was pale but seemed to be better. "Allow me to go and help Señor."

He looked into her dark eyes and brushed her hair away from her face. "Okay, but you must be careful."

She had a bundle under her arm. "I must rinse these." She said, blushing.

He nodded and motioned her to go. "Be careful." He repeated.

She gathered canteens on her arm, climbed aboard one of the saddled horses and galloped off after the others.

Tracy T. Thurman

CHAPTER THIRTEEN

Carl, Cotton, and Deke met with Bill, Pedro and Bobby. Slate and Smitty showed up soon thereafter. They rendezvoused at a predesignated place, just north of the road on some high ground, in order to regroup and assess the situation. So far all had gone as planned.

Deke sat atop a hill sweeping the road with Carl's spyglass. He saw the column as it marched along, then halted. The man with the fancy white horse and two others turned and headed out to the south. He swept the glass and saw a rider approaching them, a red cloth waving from his rifle. He slipped his way down the hill and informed the others.

Carl took the glass and looked for himself. He rubbed his whiskers. "Looks like they had another spy in the bunch, Cotton." He considered the next step. "We ain't got no horses yet. We ain't even lifted a pocket watch off these hombres." He said, contemplating.

"Let's go west a might and get a closer look. I'm thinkin' they're gonna turn and head south. We might just have to hit them there."

They moved out. Bill rolled up his sleeves, a mean expression taking shape on his features. He was ready for a fight. He was a brawler at heart and he figured it was high time some heads started getting busted. "Enough of this silly assed sneakin' around!" He exclaimed. Smitty laughed at the statement but shut up when Bill's glare caught him.

They worked their way into a position north of the column and watched. They were closer than before in lateral distance. Enough to hear Armando's furious shouts.

"Yup, them boys are plumb sick!" Slate said, peering through his glass. "Ol' Flap Jacks oughta be proud!"

Carl was watching the goings on. He agreed with Slate's assessment. He wanted to get the wagon of guns but couldn't count on it going very well. The spare horses trailed behind, all with lead ropes. It wouldn't take much to grab them and run off with them. They were some mighty fine horses. Worth a lot. He thought he'd probably keep them, though, for his own men.

The column was facing southeast. Their best angle of protective fire would be to their flanks. The chink in their armor was directly to their rear. That's also where the spare mounts were tied and that's where they would attack them.

He shared the plan with the others. "Bill, you take the right, I'll take the left. Deke, you ride next to me, then Cotton, Smitty, Bobby, Raymond, and Slate." He looked them over and saw they understood.

"Soon as we get to 'em," He added. "Smitty and Bobby, yank them horses loose and run for the hills. The rest of us'll shoot the hell out of 'em and follow you out. Pedro, I got a special job for you." Pedro sat up straight, curiosity and a shade of worry in his face.

"What is that Señor?"

Carl held up his hand as he wrote on a piece of paper. He folded it up tightly and handed it to Pedro. "Soon as we get the ball rolling with these fellas and their attention is on us, you ride like hell to the river west of Mescolare about twenty miles. Find Miguel's men and give him this note. Explain what is going on. Tell him he ain't got much time."

Pedro looked around himself and then at the others. "Why me? Why me, Señor Carl?" There was genuine fear in his eyes. That the Molina's were a frightening bunch to Pedro, Carl already knew. But the decision was made, and Pedro was the best man for the job. He told him that.

"Because, Pedro. You can ride faster than anyone else. You know the area better than anyone else, and besides... you savvy the lingo better than anyone else." He explained.

"The Molina's won't be any threat to you. You will be fine as long as you get past here. You can slip down the road a piece here and be farther away from them when the shooting starts. You won't be apt' to be seen that way. Take off after the shooting starts and don't stop 'till ya get there."

Smitty looked at the distance they needed to travel. "That's a long stretch of real estate to dodge bullets in."

Carl agreed. "Yes, it is, so you'd better keep your head down."

Slate looked in deep thought. "Ya know, that fella figures himself to be a military man, right?" The others nodded. "He's got all that fancy hardware. I'd kinda like to see him use it."

"What are ya gettin at, Slate?" Bill Grumbled.

Smitty's eyes were widening with delight as he worked Slate's idea in his own mind.

"There's a lot of ground there. Out of range, unless you had a cannon. How 'bout we line up and give that big shot a real reason to play Napoleon?"

Carl thought about it and smiled. "Awright, we'll step off and hold, just out of good rifle range and see what he does. Soon as he fires off that cannon we'll tear into 'em. If Smitty's trick works, they oughta be mighty poorly right after that."

"And if he don't...?" asked Bill.

Slate shrugged. "If he don't, then he's a fool and so am I."

******

The men returned again with the canteens. Rosaria was not with them. Armando looked for her. "Where is the woman that went with you?" He demanded.

"She was very sick, Señor, very sick. She was in the bushes and wouldn't come out. We knew you needed the water, so we hurried back. She said she would follow quickly."

Armando cursed, looking out toward the stream. He slapped his riding crop against his leg. "Okay, okay... Get these passed around and get everything back in order."

He went to the wagon where he left his map. The tailgate was a mess of spilled powder and water. He searched around but couldn't find it. He asked the woman who was working there.

"I have not seen it, Señor." Then her face grew red as a possibility of the location of his map came to her. "Some men came in a hurry to find paper for..." She turned her head away, then looked at him as if she would cry. Again, he slapped his riding crop against his leg as he stormed off.

******

Pedro walked his horse down the trail and onto the road. He led the animal a long distance to where a cut off trail pointed south and west behind a rise. He crossed himself as he climbed into the saddle and waited.

Carl, Deke, Cotton, Smitty, Bobby, Raymond, Slate, and Bill, lined up their mounts in a picket line left to right and walked them forward. There was a space of about five yards between them. They walked to the road and waited. Eight men, eight horses, eight guns.

Carl looked down the line. Deke was noticeably edgy, but eager. Smitty bit off a piece of chewing tobacco and offered it to Bobby who declined. Bobby looked nervous, but ready. Cotton and Slate looked cool as a stone, expressionless, but for their searching eyes. Bill's jaw was set tight in a characteristic sneer. It was as close to a smile as usually got.

******

"Señor! Señor!" came a shout from a man at the back of the column. "Señor!" He called again.

Armando looked to where he pointed and saw the figures of mounted men lined up in the distance. He looked again in disbelief, using his spyglass. "Well, it looks like our gringo saboteurs have grown a backbone!" He hurried his pace as he moved about. He scanned the area around them, then counted. Eight men? Is that all there is?! They must be suicidal!"

He stepped away from his column, turned, and glanced a battle line of his own. Time was not on his side. He knew that. But he could not resist this opportunity to demonstrate his military prowess.

"Twenty men! You there! Line up! Prepare for battle! Bring the cannon forward!"

Without hesitation, the men complied. They, too, were ready for some form of action. Though they were weakened from sickness, they were ready to fight. The cannon moved into position in the center of the line. The cannon crew readied their weapon, setting its angle and elevation to fire upon the riders. "What load do you wish, Señor?" The cannoneer asked.

Armando looked again through his glass and estimated the range. They were just out of effective rifle range. "Grapeshot double the load." He commanded.

The cannoneer complied. The weapon was loaded and ready.

Carl watched through his glass. "Damn ain't them boys sharp?" He stated. "There's twenty on the line there. That's half his force. Do your best to make your shots count." The men all nodded. Bobby swallowed hard and dried his hands on his pants.

Carl looked over at Deke.

Deke returned his look and nodded. He nudged his horse forward in a slow walk prompting the rest to move as well.

Armando saw them begin to advance. He swelled his chest and stood tall. *'This will be a good rehearsal for when I catch Miguel,'* he thought. He drew his saber and held it high. He looked right and left at his men now in a kneeling position, their rifles at the ready. The cannon crew stood by, beaming with pride, as they were about to demonstrate their beloved artillery piece.

Armando waited a second more. Raul Molina will love to hear this story and I will be rewarded greatly. "Ready!" He called out. Silence pervaded a moment longer. He dropped his saber sharply pointing it directly at the enemy... "FIRE!" The cannoneer touched the torch to the fuse...

Carl halted when he saw the saber drop. A long second went by. Then... The cannon appeared to leap into the air and shatter in an ear bursting detonation! KABOOM!!! The explosion was deafening! A violent, metallic eruption of searing hot fragments exploded in the place where the weapon stood. Burning debris scattered fifty yards in every direction. The rear wagon was set aflame as the fiery particles rained down on the white canvas cover. Men, and pieces of men, were flung into the air like hellish confetti. The entire column fell to the ground. Horses screamed and fought at their harnesses. A great cloud of smoke rose high into the air then spread out like a mushroom. It seemed the entire earth screamed and died. There was a gaping hole in the ground, men and horses lay scattered like toys a child had tossed away.

Armando was thrown from his position, bits of hot metal slammed into the side of his face and down his torso. Searing pain shot through him. The world went black as he tumbled and fell. His head felt like a great gong had been rung inside it. He could hear only his own breathing and heartbeat. Everything was spinning wildly around him. He could feel nothing else but the stunned silence that swept over him.

******

The concussion from the explosion hit them in the chest like a giant fist. Their horses bucked and strained at their bits. Bobby hung on to his pommel for dear life trying to settle his mount down. "Holy shit, Smitty!" Slate called out. "How much did you put in that thing?!"

Smitty had the wind knocked out of him. He shrugged and gasped, getting his air back. "Apparently, just enough!"

Bill laughed out loud. Which was as much a shock as the concussion itself.

Carl gritted his teeth. "Let's go!"

He spurred his horse hard. With an exuberant shout, the others did the same. They raced toward the destruction leaning low against their horses' necks. Bill fired first.

Deke's pistol was out and ready, he saw a man raise to his feet. He pulled the trigger, the Colt bucked in his hand and the man toppled over backwards. A man raised his rifle, the Colt bucked again, and he crumpled over onto his face. They rode hard and fast. Shouting and shooting, teeth gritted, fire burning fiercely in their narrowed eyes.

Bobby jerked as a bullet slammed into him. He dropped his gun as he recoiled from the impact. Regaining his seat, he yanked his other pistol and rejoined the fight.

They grew nearer by the second. The men at the column were still rocked by the explosion. They tried to regroup. Others rushed to the line and fired their rifles as rapidly as they could load them. They were panicked. Their shots were going wild. The men bore down on them. Armando's men fell and then others fell next to them; some dropped their rifles and ran away.

Viciously spurring their mounts onward, they burst through what remained of the line with the ferocity of a thunderstorm.

Bobby was wounded, he couldn't dismount to get the horses. Raymond saw the problem and jumped to help Smitty. In a second the horses were loosened from the wagon and galloping back behind Smitty's and Raymond's horses.

Bobby held on as he spun his mount around. He was growing light headed, but knew he had to hang on with everything he had.

Deke and Carl swept the side of the column raking fire into the wagons and among the men who were either scrambling for their weapons or trying to just get out of the way. Cotton followed right behind them, firing as he went. Slate and Bill did the same on the other side. Firing their guns and yelling with blood in their faces, lathered up into a killing frenzy. They wheeled around and charged back the way they came. Bill's pistols were empty, He yanked a coach gun from a scabbard, leveled it with one arm, and fired into groups of men as he thundered by. Deke saw the man who had raised his saber stagger to his feet. He bore down on him. A thousand pounds of horse flesh slammed into him with the force of a freight train.

Armando struggled to his feet. His saber was gone. He swayed in place. The noise of the battle encapsulated him. The sky seemed to tumble to the earth. He reached for his side arm but couldn't lift it.

Just then he was knocked violently to the ground. Hooves thundered by him as he lay in the dirt, his mouth agape, his eyes staring into the stars that swirled in front of them.

They ran their horses back to the hills whooping and hollering. Deke rammed his pistols back in their holsters relishing in the sound of gunfire ringing in his ears and the sulphuric smell of burned gunpowder in his nose. His horse ran like it could go on forever. They cleared the road and pulled up only a few yards farther. They turned to assess the results of the attack.

The column sat in disarray, a black hole spread from where the cannon had been. They saw men stumble and fall. Then rise up and stumble to the wagons. The rear wagon was burning, almost fully engulfed by this time.

"I reckon the fight's gone out of them boys!" Cotton exclaimed.

The men were breathing hard, the horses panted. Bill tore at his sleeve and tied off a bullet wound in his upper arm. Carl had a gash across his left cheek that would likely need stitches. Slate, Cotton, and Deke were mostly unscathed. Smitty's leg bled where a bullet had torn through the flesh. Raymond leaned over in his saddle clutching his left hand, broken from being tangled in the horses' ropes.

Bobby reined up next to Deke and looked over at him. His face was pale, he managed an awkward smile, then wavered in his seat, and toppled to the ground. Deke jumped from his saddle and knelt next to his friend. The front of his shirt was blood soaked. Slate elbowed in and tore the garment away. A jagged hole bled profusely from high in the center of his chest. Bobby coughed a couple of times, looked up at them and died.

Carl surveyed the men shaking his head. "Bobby was a good man, a young man. But what's done is done." They gave much worse than they received. "Load him up on his horse. Let's round up the horses we took and get the hell out of here!"

The words fell heavy on the men, especially Deke. Bobby was the first friend he ever had. He would miss him terribly. When they got him on his horse, secured in place, Deke laid his hand on the back of Bobby's head.

"I'll make you sure you get a decent burial, pard. I sure will." His eyes burned and grew cloudy, the back of his neck ached. He hadn't shed a single tear since before he could remember. He wasn't about to do it now. He tried with all his might anyhow.

Carl thought of saying something to him but decided to leave him be. A man finds his own way to mourn the loss of a friend, and he would let Deke do that in his own way.

******

Pedro's horse jumped at the sound of the explosion. He spurred the animal onward, sitting low in the saddle, lashing its hind quarters with a long leather quirt. He sped on, urging the animal faster as he rode. He picked his trail carefully guiding his way through the scrub brush. He clamped his knees and held tight. The sound of the battle raged in the distance and quickly fell behind him.

"Come on, my friend," He whispered to his horse. "We have a long way to go and we can't get caught before we get there."

******

Two men lifted Armando by his shoulders. The wounds that penetrated the left side of his face dripped blood. His clothes were bloody in several places where they had been punctured by shrapnel from the exploding cannon. His right arm appeared to be broken. They dragged him to the shade of a tree and poured water over his face.

Maria rushed to his side dabbing, at the wounds, inspecting them and trying to remove the jagged pieces of metal. He winced and pulled away. His eyes fluttered, and his head seemed to swirl in a circle. He tried to speak but couldn't. A loud ring persisted painfully in his ears.

The woman held a spoon to his mouth and tried to get him to swallow some medicine. He choked on it. She tried again, until she got most of it in him. She lifted his arm and shook her head. She whispered frantic prayers.

The two men who carried him over watched her in her work. When she looked at his arm, they knew what they had to do. The woman took a deep breath. While the men held him, she pulled with all her might snapping the bone back into place. Armando cried out in pain, gritted his teeth and squeezed his eyes shut. He remained drifting, in and out of consciousness, as they continued working on him.

There were moans from the wounded, the other women tended to them as best they could. The burning wagon collapsed in its place. Men were scurrying about, trying to catch horses that had broken loose from their tethers. Other horses were injured and had to be shot. There were dead men scattered here and there that had to be retrieved, identified, and buried.

Tracy T. Thurman

CHAPTER FOURTEEN

"Señor!" Miguel turned to look where the man pointed. A rider galloped toward them. Miguel strained his eyes to see. Juan handed him his spyglass. Expanding it, Miguel raised to his eye. A look of surprise and disbelief came to his face. He handed the glass back to Juan. "Look, brother..."

Juan scanned the landscape until the rider was centered in view. "I'll be damned!" He said and let out a joyous laugh.

They kicked their mounts into a gallop to intercept the rider.

Rosaria clung to the saddle. She was in bad shape when they came to her. She fell into their arms. The ride had taken a hard toll on her after suffering from the sickness.

"Quickly, let's get her water and some shade." They carried her to where the rest of the men and mules were. They strung a tarp up and propped her up under it. She drank little sips of water at first, then great drinks until she coughed on it. Juan handed her some bread. "Eat something. You'll feel better."

She looked at them and smiled. "Oh, how I have missed you both, cousins!" They grinned at her, glad to see her as well.

"I have much to tell you." She reached inside her blouse and withdrew Armando's map.

She told her story, turning her head in shame at what she had done. The two brothers scoffed at it. "You are a courageous woman!" they exclaimed. "A man sacrifices his life and he is dead. You have sacrificed much more than that. It will never be mentioned again. You are a hero of the Molina Rancho and that is what you will always be."

Miguel studied the map. It wasn't much different than his own except it showed the course in which Armando intended to take to intercept him. "He will have advanced riders out, always two." She warned. Then she paused and spoke softly. "He intends to carry your heads back to Raul in a sack."

Miguel took a deep breath and exhaled slowly. "He is not only arrogant, but foolish as well. We shall see whose head is delivered to Raul..."

He rolled up the map and tapped Juan with it. "We will be waiting." He said with a confident wink.

Juan pointed at three men. Ride out and watch for anyone approaching. You there, you there, and you there." He pointed the directions in which he wanted them to go. "Don't shoot if you don't have to. Bring them in alive if you can."

The three rode as they were directed, tipping their sombreros deeply as they passed Rosaria. The courtesy pleased her.

They decided to make their camp where they were. Rosario was in no shape to ride farther that day. They knew where Armando was and where he would be as he traveled. There was no reason to hurry.

In the night as they sat by the firelight a voice called from the dark. It was one of the men Juan had sent out earlier. "Señor, I am coming in with a prisoner."

Another voice echoed after the first. "I am no prisoner, you horse's ass!"

Miguel shrugged. "Come in to the light." He said.

Juan's outrider entered the firelight, pulling Pedro by his sleeve. Pedro jerked away from him, cursing him in the process.

Miguel studied him. "You are Pedro, one of Señor Ferguson's men."

Pedro nodded sweeping his sombrero from his head. "Si, that is right, Señor Molina."

"You have news?"

"Si"

"Speak, my friend, speak." Miguel prompted him.

Pedro began telling of everything that had happened, including sabotaging the weapons and the water. He told of the battle that took place as he was leaving and the loud explosion he assumed was the cannon. When he was done he asked for a drink of water.

Miguel handed him a canteen, apologizing for not offering sooner.

The two brothers exchanged glances.

"Carl and his men have done us a great favor." Juan said.

"Yes. I think we should take the men we have and carry the fight to Armando. Catch him while he is still licking his wounds." Miguel suggested.

Juan agreed. "We can leave a guard detail here."

Miguel shook his head. "No, we will bring it with us. We will meet Armando and show it to him before we kill him. Then we will go to the Hacienda without having to go through those mountains.

Miguel turned to Pedro. "You are a good man, Pedro. Would you like to ride with us?"

Pedro looked about, "You mean ride with you? The Molina Rancho?"

Miguel laughed, "Of course, my friend."

Pedro placed his sombrero back on his head. "I have to return to Señor Ferguson. I will fight with you. But then I must return."

Miguel nodded his head. "I understand. But know that you have my respect and gratitude." He reached his hand out.

Pedro blinked his eyes, then shook hands with Miguel Molina. "Gracias, Señor Molina, gracias." He stepped away from the firelight then, found his horse and looked for a place to bed down for the night. If he had of been handed a stack of gold bars it wouldn't have made more of an impression.

******

Armando was conscious. He felt pain throughout his entire body. His ears still rang persistently. His arm was in a sling, a bandage wrapped about his head. He hobbled about, doing his best to stand straight. Surveying the damage, he felt the growing pangs of defeat. He tried to put it out of his mind. He thought he was only suffering the effects of his wounds.

The Sergeant was dead, his body obliterated by the detonation of the cannon. He selected another. "Have my horse brought to me. Get the men mounted up and get moving. We still have a job to do. We will return and exact our revenge on these gringos afterward!"

The new Sergeant stepped off barking orders. The woman, Maria, who had tended his injuries walked to him with a bowl of salve to dab on the wounds on his face. He waited for her, smiling as best he could. She looked at him sadly. Her constantly whispered prayers intensifying as she treated him.

When she was done he placed his hand on her shoulders. "I am deeply indebted to you, Señora." She smiled and started to turn away. He stopped her. "Where is Rosaria?" He asked. The woman looked down she held her hand up indicating he should wait where he was. She returned quickly, handing him a jagged strip of blue material. The same material Rosaria's skirt was made of.

"Those bastards took her!" His face swelled in anger. "What kind of men are these? I will kill them all when I return!" He placed the torn fabric inside his shirt. Maria held her hand up again. He nodded, growing impatient. She walked to the tree where she had tended him, reached behind it, and returned.

She looked up at him smiling, from behind the folds of her dress, she produced his saber. He thought it was lost, never to be found. It gleamed brilliantly in the sunlight, he held it up admiring it, grateful to have it back. There were a few scratches that could easily be repaired, but it was otherwise straight and strong as ever.

The woman beamed proudly at him. "Gracias, Señora, muchas gracias!" He bent down and kissed her on the cheek. Her hand went to the place where he kissed her. A tear of joy dripped from her eye.

Armando climbed into his saddle. He gritted his teeth at the pain, raised his left arm high, then brought it down. The column began moving once again. He looked back committing this place to memory. "I will return, and this ground will soak up the blood of those who did this."

******

Miguel and Juan led their men northward to intercept Armando's company. From what Pedro had told them they must have suffered enough damage to have reduced their force and fighting ability substantially.

"Pity about the cannon brother..." Miguel said.

"Why is that?" Juan replied.

"I was hoping to keep it..."

"We can find another, my brother, we can find another..."

Rosaria rode in back. They saddled a horse for her and gave her blankets to make it more comfortable. A gun belt with two pistols hung on the pommel. She did not complain. She only looked forward to seeing this thing done. It had gone on too long and cost too many lives.

Miguel called Pedro to the front. "Do you know how Señor Ferguson made out after their fight?"

Pedro shook his head, a look of worry on his face. "No, Señor, I was not there, He told me to come here instead."

"I am sure they are all fine. We will see them soon and have a great fiesta!"

Pedro nodded and forced a smile. "Yes, that would be good, very good." Pedro felt awkward riding with these men. "Señor, I would like to ride out ahead and see what's coming."

Miguel agreed. "Take another man with you. Do not be seen."

Pedro wheeled his horse around and pointed to a vaquero he knew as a friendly one. "You go with me."

The two galloped ahead.

******

As Armando rode, his mind collected the thoughts of the journey. It looked like it had become a dismal failure. He cursed himself for not discovering the sabotage sooner. Raul would not be pleased at losing his cannon or the many men and horses that were lost. He brought his mount around suddenly. "Keep moving, be on your guard."

He waited for the weapons wagon to approach his position. "Get in the back, disassemble the Gatling gun and inspect it. Look at everything that is there!"

He rode by the rest of the column. "Keep on the lookout!" He ordered, catching up to the weapons wagon, he paced his horse alongside. Presently one of the armorers poked his head out from beneath the cover. He held a broken rod in his hand. "This was in one of the barrels, Señor!"

Armando sneered. "Those bastards..." He spat. "We will use that gun to slaughter Miguel and his men. Then we will return and use it to slaughter those gringos who attacked us yesterday."

******

Pedro and his companion came to the top of a rise that allowed a commanding view of the terrain around it. "This would be a good place to fight." Pedro said.

The other man looked around and agreed. "If the Raul's are coming here, it would. We don't know for sure yet." They scanned the land before them. "Let's wait and watch from here."

Within an hour they saw the rising dust that told of a procession traveling their direction. "It has to be the Raul's!" The vaquero said. "Si, it is." The two turned back to where Miguel was and carried the news. Pedro described the rise where they watched, recommending it as a place to take their position.

Miguel studied the map Rosaria brought. "Armando must not have been aware she got away with this or he would have changed his plan." As it was, he followed the exact course marked in pencil. "Surely he can't be that foolish."

"We will set up there, where Pedro suggested, two lines of men with rifles. We will keep the horses and mules in the back behind the rise where they won't be in danger. I want to capture as many of them alive as we can." He stated. "If we can convince them to surrender, we won't have to kill so many of them. Armando will wish he was killed."

They did as he described, reaching the area just as the dust from the approaching column was growing evident, and the forms of men and wagons could be seen as dots coming over the horizon. Miguel sent men out to the flanks, sharpshooters to lay low and fire with pinpoint effect. They raised a large red banner emblazoned with gold "M" with a rising sun over the top and waited.

Armando's two advanced riders returned in a run. "Señor! They are in place ahead up on a rise. Directly in our path!"

It was not what he expected. He thought he would have to chase Miguel and overtake him. *'Now here he is. He must have known somehow that I was coming this way. A spy.'* He thought. *'A spy must have slipped away during the fight and ran to tell them.'* His anger swelled up even more.

He galloped his horse ahead far enough to see the forms on the hill and the red banner that fluttered above them. He rode back. "Very well, if this is where he chooses to die then so be it! He has only made my job easier!"

"Bring out the Patron's banner!" He ordered. "Prepare yourselves for battle! Miguel has made our chase shorter!"

The weapons wagon was stripped of its cover, Ammunition was distributed. The Gatling gun made ready. Armando called to his sergeant. "See that every man and woman has a rifle and a side arm, every one of them!"

He called another man. "Post the banner on your stirrup! You have the honor to carry the rightful crest into battle!" The man sat up straight in his saddle and saluted, he grabbed the banner as it was being brought forward from the weapons wagon. He unfurled it, posted it in right stirrup and took his place at the head of the column. Armando removed the sling from his arm and threw it away, directing Maria to wrap his arm heavily and tightly. He worked his hand and fingers as she did so. Her whispered prayers provided accompaniment to her work.

******

"They will use the Gatling gun at the center of their line." Miguel said.

Juan agreed. "Pedro said they sabotaged it. Maybe we'll get to see it blow up?"

Miguel shook his head. "No, I think Armando would have thought to have it inspected after the cannon. I would have. I would have checked everything."

The lines were set. Armando placed his men in position. The Gatling gun was, indeed, posted in the center. Juan looked at the men in front of him and to his sides. "You there, you five mule tenders..." The men looked up with an expression of dread. "To the front. Where you belong, the front, NOW!" He ordered.

The men got up and moved forward. "Keep your aim sharp, and you'll have nothing to worry about!" He called to them.

The wind snapped at the banners. Horses stomped nervously. Long moments passed as men glared at each other over a distance no farther than a strong man could throw a rock.

Armando looked to his left and to his right. The men on the Gatling gun were to open fire at the drop of his saber.

He looked straight ahead with a hate filled scowl. He raised his saber and sharply brought it down.

The man on the gun leaned into the handle that turned the barrels and brought them into firing position. He pushed hard, just as a shot rang out from his left. He never heard it however, because it was intended for him. He sagged and fell over the back side of the wagon.

Armando raised his saber again and slashed it down furiously. The second man grasped the handle, inched it forward when the next shot delivered him the same fate as the first man. "Fire! Dammit! FIRE!" Armando yelled. His men cut loose with a volley from their rifles. Miguel shouted to his men "GO!" They dug their spurs into the flanks of their mounts and charged!

The men in the flanks rose and began firing at will. Another man got the Gatling gun and started cranking it wildly. The gun fired in the manner it was designed. He swept it left and right tearing down riders and horses as he did. Juan's mule tenders fell in the first volley.

Miguel kicked his horse forward at a wild run. He held his pistol extended. He fired, then fired again. The man on the Gatling gun fell away.

Enrique stood in his stirrups, firing his pistol in one hand, swinging his sabre with the other. He charged his horse into the oncoming assault, cutting a swath through them, then turning and charging back again.

Miguel called to him. "Get a rope on the gun and pull it away!"

Enrique stowed his pistol, shook out his lariat and swung a wide loop toward it. A bullet from Armando's gun crashed through his ribs and exploded his heart. He toppled over the rear of horse and lay still, his sword lying bloodstained in the grass beside him.

Miguel screamed in rage!

Pedro jammed his pistol back in his holster. He leaned from the saddle and scooped up Enrique's lariat; he swung it wide and flung it hard at the gun. The loop slapped itself around the weapon like a flying snake grabbing its prey. He yanked it hard, dallying a fast hitch on his pommel and jabbed his spurs into his horse's flank. The animal jumped, dug its hooves in, and jerked the weapon free from the wagon, sending it crashing to the ground. Pedro cast the rope away, drew his pistol and drove back into the fight.

A man wearing a yellow sash leapt from his saddle and grabbed Pedro around the neck, pulling him violently from his horse. The two men fought gouging and kicking. The man swung a broken rifle at Pedro's head. Pedro ducked, grabbing his knife as he did, coming up with a vicious slash that cut deep across the man's face, as he doubled over in pain, Pedro thrust the knife blade deep into the man's chest, sinking it to the hilt through his breast bone. Pedro yanked the blade free and spun around, crouched low, he grabbed another man and buried the blade once again.

Juan spurred his mount hard to the left of the line. He fired as he went cursing the men in front of him. He emptied his pistol, grabbed his other one and drove through the melee, firing into every yellow sash that entered his field of view. The weapon clicked on a spent cartridge. He flipped it around and bludgeoned the next man who fell before him. Kicking his feet free from the stirrups, he yanked his knife from its sheath, then drew a saber with his other hand and waded into the fight with the ferocity of a mad man.

Men were clashing their horses, leaping on each other with knives and lances, firing their guns at point blank range until they were empty, then turning them to use as clubs. The field was a confusion of red and yellow sashes stained by blood. Savage screams of fury blended with screams of mortal agony.

Armando gritted his teeth and growled wildly, He slashed his saber down with his left arm while firing his pistol with his right. Every shot sent a stab of pain through his arm, but adrenaline and a feverish desire to kill pushed it from his mind. A man fell beneath his blade with a bloody gash that opened his skull.

Miguel pointed his pistol at him, bearing down with the intent of crushing him. Armando saw him coming, he yelled viciously. He charged at him waving his blood dripping saber high above his head, his teeth bared, screaming for Miguel's blood at the top of his lungs.

Miguel fired. The bullet shattered Armando's left shoulder blade. He flew from his horse. Crashing to the ground in a heap. He tried to get up but fell again. His left arm hung useless at his side, his right worked, but the fracture was aggravated to the point that it wouldn't hold him up. Extreme pain shot through his body. He looked about and saw his men falling or lying dead. He looked to the sky as it swirled around him and he sank to his knees.

The fighting subsided. Only a few reports echoed then stopped all together. The ground was littered with dead and dying men.

Armando shook his head and staggered to his feet. Blood trickled from his wounds, his shoulder hung as if it had been detached from his body, his right arm trembled involuntarily. He picked up his saber and stabbed it into the ground. He spat hatefully and stood where he was.

Miguel stepped his horse past him without acknowledging him. He stood in his stirrups. "You men! You women! All of you! This fight is over! There is no reason to die! Drop your weapons! All of you! You will not be harmed!"

The sound of rifles and gun belts being dropped echoed from the battle lines. Yellow sashes were being taken off and cast away.

Miguel called to two men who hung their heads in defeat. "You will be alright. You will live. Get some others and bring your wagons. All of them. Do not do anything foolish!"

They did as they were told. The wagons moved forward. Miguel's men moved about them pulling the women out as they did so, inspecting the contents.

Maria ran to Armando tears streaming down her face. She muttered her prayers more intensely than ever before.

Juan and the others converged on the scene. Rosaria sat her horse and accompanied them. Armando saw her coming and gasped. "Rosaria! I thought you were..." Then it became clear. His eyes narrowed as the cold hand of betrayal gripped his heart. He yelled at her furiously. "You treacherous whore!"

She held her head up and scowled at him. "You are a small man Armando, in every way." Miguel and Juan laughed, jeering at him. Maria stood by his side, then moved to his right muttering in his ear. She cried profusely while she dabbed at his wounds. He felt the gun folded in her skirt.

Miguel glared at him hatefully, then swept his arms around. "All of this? All of this! Is it worth it to you?!" He held Armando in a bitter stare. "Will we hang you, or drag you to death?"

Armando looked up at him as his fingers closed on the butt of the gun. He smiled. Then broke into a laugh. "You will do neither." He raised the gun to his chin and pulled the trigger.

His body jumped, then fell to the ground, convulsed, and died. Maria wailed mournfully and fell to her knees at his side. Hands clasped, she rocked back and forth, sobbing out her prayers in desperation.

Miguel shook his head. He turned to go.

Maria picked up the gun. It was huge in her trembling hands. She pointed it at Miguel, closed her eyes tightly... then Rosaria shot her.

CHAPTER FIFTEEN

Deke's clothes were covered with dirt. The grave on the top of the hill was deep. Slate and some of the others offered to help but it was a chore he wanted to do on his own. He gathered a big pile of smooth stones from the creek bed and a few items of Bobby's he thought he would like to take if he could.

He laid his friend gently in the bottom wrapped in cloth head to toe. He placed his own gun belt next to him, set his boots in by his feet, laid his hat on his chest, a small bottle of whiskey and an old tin can shot full of holes.

"I traded ya gun belts." Deke said. "I figured ya wouldn't mind. Your guns are lying out there in the dirt somewhere. I kept the concho Carl gave me though and added it to yours." He paused and rubbed his forearm across his eyes. "I'll swap ya back, next time I see ya…"

He knelt down and tried to remember a prayer his mother taught him long ago. He recalled the memory, that's the best he could do. He stood, and took a deep, deep breath. "Ride easy, pard. Ride easy…"

He shoveled the dirt, working into the night. There were moments when he stopped and sat on his knees next to the grave and spoke to his friend some more. Then he'd get to his feet with another deep breath and go back to work.

When he was done. The moon was high, illuminating everything in a soft glow. He piled the stones on top, arranging them just right. Then sat there, talking to Bobby, watching the moon make its way across the sky.

******

Raymond came riding through the gap fast. He hollered "Pedro's back!" He turned and raced back to where his friend was coming through leading a pack mule. Carl stepped out to meet him as did Bill and Cotton.

Pedro stepped from the saddle and led the animals to where the big table was. He removed some ropes and a tarp and lifted a very old looking chest from the mule. He sat it on the table, "Miguel Molina told me to give this to you." He said to Carl, then trailed his animals to the corral.

Cotton watched him go curiously. "Well, don't ya wanna see what's in it?"

Pedro waved his hand over his shoulder. "You see for yourselves. I'm tired and hungry."

Tracy T. Thurman

CHAPTER SIXTEEN

A loud knock sounded on the great oaken doors of the Rancho De Molina hacienda. A servant woman opened the door only to find a box. She carried it inside and called to Señor Raul Molina.

He examined the box, turning it in all directions. His wife joined him. "Open it!" she urged. He opened the box, removing the paper that covered the contents. He stepped back in shock and terror when he saw the gaping face of Armando Agulier staring up at him! His wife screamed, then fainted in a heap.

Outside, shots rang out, then more. Men were yelling. He heard the sounds of running boots and crashing hooves. Then he could hear the distinct sound of a Gatling gun being fired. He took a long-barreled revolver from a drawer, a Colt Navy .44, sat down in a big leather chair, and waited.

******

Deke walked his horse back to the corral as the sun was coming up on a new day. He heard Flap Jacks rustling around in the mess tent, the smell of coffee brewing told him Flap Jacks was getting breakfast ready. The cattle were lowing out on the range, the grass was wet with dew. A damp mist hung in the air. He leaned against the rail, chin resting on his crossed arms. He didn't know what the future held, only that the gun belt on his hips fit well and that was something he was sure he was born to.

Other Books
By
Tracy T. Thurman

Outlaw Brand: Hell to Pay

Outlaw Brand: The Thin Line

The Guns of the Broke Knife Mine

Whiskey Trail

Made in the USA
Lexington, KY
03 May 2019